DO THEY HAVE A
PILL FOR THAT?

DO THEY HAVE A PILL FOR THAT?

A Psychologist's Story

T.L. Shull

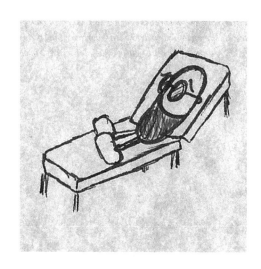

iUniverse®

DO THEY HAVE A PILL FOR THAT?
A PSYCHOLOGIST'S STORY

iUniverse books may be ordered through booksellers or by contacting:

iUniverse
1663 Liberty Drive
Bloomington, IN 47403
www.iuniverse.com
1-800-Authors (1-800-288-4677)

Because of the dynamic nature of the Internet, any web addresses or links contained in this book may have changed since publication and may no longer be valid. The views expressed in this work are solely those of the author and do not necessarily reflect the views of the publisher, and the publisher hereby disclaims any responsibility for them.

Any people depicted in stock imagery provided by Getty Images are models, and such images are being used for illustrative purposes only. Certain stock imagery © Getty Images.

ISBN: 978-1-5320-6975-8 (sc)
ISBN: 978-1-5320-7050-1 (e)

Library of Congress Control Number: 2019902469

Print information available on the last page.

iUniverse rev. date: 03/08/2019

DEDICATION

I dedicate this book to the memory of my compassionate father, whose inspiration touched lives, and whom never got a chance to see this work that he so strongly advocated for.

ACKNOWLEDGMENTS

To my wife and children who tolerated my neurosis while I was seven years in writing this book.

To all my patients and their laughter and pain, their troubles and triumphs, may they all find peace and mental health. This is their story, not mine.

DOES ANYONE HAVE A PILL FOR THAT?

CHAPTER ONE

He was literally the red haired stepchild. He had piercing blue eyes and a serene, calm affect, which beguiled the inner torment he felt. He was, at just seven years old a very good looking young freckled faced Irish boy. He was also very troubled on what was to be his last day. He tearfully walked over to his small desk and pulled out a picture of his father, who died at only 34 years of age of heart failure one year previously. He was close to his father and missed him terribly. His father was deeply religious and believed in God and Heaven, and so did little Peter. Everyone called him Pedee however for unknown reasons. He took the picture, gently kissed it, and then put it in his pocket. He then walked slowly, but deliberately to a drawer at his desk, where some of his father's belongings were, one of which was his father's belt. When stretched out the belt was almost two feet more than Pedee was standing. He then took the belt out and pulled his little chair out from under his desk positioning it in his clothes closet, under the bar which held the clothes. For someone so small and delicate he was able to calmly tie the belt around the bar and stood on the chair tightly tying the other end around his neck. As if to gasp his last breath he hesitated a moment, then stepped off the chair. He wiggled terribly on the belt, for what seemed like hours at first, as the oxygen was cut off with the blood supply to his little brain. Then he was motionless, anoxia set in and his face mirrored the blue rose that sat on his desk, due to lack of oxygen. Curiously, when his stepmother and his three older stepbrothers came in to find him hanging, there were no cries or shrieks. One called the emergency number. Despite their best efforts Pedee was gone, the EMT's could not resuscitate.

Pedee exemplified the story of Cinderella. His father married a domineering woman, whose older children emotionally abused him, and who he had conflicts with over parenting issues. When he died Pedee was open to be abused without protection. He was however, quiet about his pain, internalizing it. No one in the

1

neighborhood knew anything as it was a family secret, and people never really saw too much of Pedee as he mainly stayed inside after school. Even his teachers were blind and picked up on nothing at school. They just saw him as shy and withdrawn, isolative, quiet and not playing too much with other children. He was bright, but after the death of his father his grades dropped, but again, no one questioned and Pedee slipped through the cracks.

The kids next door tried to engage him in play when he was allowed to come out, but he shied away. He looked on from a distance when they flew their model planes, and played whiffle ball in their backyard, probably longing to play but fearing repercussions.

The kids next door did not understand why he acted the way he did, they could not put it all together. Of course they too would eventually undergo abuse themselves in the very near future by a tyrannical stepfather. Their father however would succumb not to death but by being exiled from the household by their mother, only to be replaced by her choice of a tyrannical and egomaniacal miscreant who relished terror tactics as a way to discipline.

The children next door were oblivious to the horrible tragedy that unfolded next door.

They did notice that there was an ambulance outside the house next door, but did not put it together that it had anything to do with little Pedee. They did report this to their mother who was later told that Pedee hung himself. She inquired as to how this came about and Pedee's stepmother told their mother that Pedee was psychologically mentally ill. The family was concerned about him the stepmother told the children's mother, but also told her that they had tried to get him counseling but he resisted. He became more depressed after his father died his stepmother told their mother again. She told my mother that she and her sons were very sad at Pedee's suicide. The children's mother came back and explained to the children's father that the stepmother did not appear to be very distressed by this.

The father was very saddened by this event. They both felt that there was more to this than met the eye.

The neighborhood thereafter became strangely quiet. The kids used to play street hockey in front of Pedee's house, but now they played hockey down the street at some other kid's house.

It was as if this house represented death, and took the life of an innocent.

The kids seemed to sense and fear the dark force within the house that seemed to absorb the life force of a child that was misunderstood by all. The child who was exiled, berated, emotionally abused and vilified as different by a stepfamily who did not identify him as one of them.

The sad part of all this was that he was an invisible child, that no one at school noticed, or the neighborhood even cared to notice. He was a cipher in humanity. Pedee was very sensitive however and in order to survive became invisible or as invisible as much as he could be. He was hiding in plain sight. However, the pain was overwhelming and he could not contain it any further, thus his escape. It is only hoped that he has finally found the peace he sought, and so rightfully deserved.

The children next door went on with life, distracting themselves from the tragic circumstance next door. They were back at it again. Their large, and very green tank slowly rolled across an uneven surface to acquire its' target. It proceeded as quietly as a tank could so as not to alert the enemy. Above at a higher point, the spotter with binoculars quietly called out over his walkie talkie

"Target ahead" to the tank driver below.

The tank driver responded immediately "Target in sight."

The spotter stated back, "Fire when ready."

Quietly, as to himself, the driver said, "Now five degrees to starboard, and three degrees' elevation."

Then as if Mount Vesuvius just erupted, a thunderous explosion was heard, as the tank cannon erupted in white smoke. Target acquired and eliminated---a successful hit, as witnessed through the binoculars by the spotter above. Both the tank driver, hiding behind the couch that drove the remote control tank was gone, as was his brother from the top of the stairs acting as a spotter. When their mother bent over to sort the laundry the brothers plotted the destruction of her buttocks. She yelled out rubbing her butt as a very large circle of white powder outlined the decimated area.

The boys laughed, and said in unison, "War is hell."

Later they would catch hell by their father. Later, that evening, their World War Two veteran father, who bought them the tank, told them that this was "an unacceptable use of military equipment, requiring a confinement to quarters for two days." He then congratulated the boys on successful target elimination. He then winked at them.

The next day he let them out again and told mother that "Boys will be boys, and that they learned their lesson."

My father was very forgiving, gentle and kind. He did not believe in using corporal punishment, thank God. The following year he bought us a toy 30 caliber machine gun, for which my brother and I assaulted my mother and grandparents with. Again, he confined us to our quarters then learned his lesson: don't buy us weapons of mass destruction. From then on he bought us model airplanes knowing that they were not radio controlled so we could not put into action an aerial assault on my mother. He also flew the models we made and then we crashed them because we sucked as pilots. My father wanted to be a pilot in the war but his ears were bad and he was not good in math. However, he did make sergeant in the army and was wounded in the war. He rarely talked about the war. He'd asked us to be kind to all we encounter because life, he explained is short and it can be hard, as he'd had seen a world of war.

He used to say, "Boys we are only here for a visit so make the best of every day."

During the sixties growing up in a large city, my brother and I became interested in ice hockey. We played for the park district and loved the Blackhawks. I especially liked Stan Mikita. I went to several games with my dad and always marveled at the way they skated and manipulated the puck. I loved hockey but not the fights. I injured my back in a practice game and "retired" from the game permanently. I grieved the loss of a game I loved so much. My dad took us to aviation movies, like *The Great Waldo Pepper* with Robert Redford. He did tell us one story where he entered a Japanese naval air station but it was riddled with 50 caliber bullets because previously it had been strafed by P-51 mustangs. He did not say too much afterward about it, rarely talking about his war experiences. He tried to shelter us from the violence amidst The Vietnam War. But some of the biggest wars penetrate our homes, being fought on the home front. He was glad we missed it as we entered high school, saving us from experiencing the things he had endured and still did not verbalize.

Then, our world caved in. My mother declared she was divorcing my father. Apparently "dating" someone from her work that she felt was more interesting than my father. Our father was a loving husband and incredible father. He was always here for her and for us too. Worn down from the woes of war and raising two high energy sons, he was tired, not always having the gumption to take his wife out on the town. This behavior was unacceptable to my mother who let my father know he was not doing enough. He worked overtime to give her everything he possibly could.

Like the crust of the Earth broken and shattered after an earthquake, so was my father's heart. He faced his sons wanting to be strong for us, holding back his tears. But the pain overwhelmed us all, and my brother and I saw those tears. My father made us boys a promise he would still see us, we could still be with him. He said we'd work it out, that it'd all be okay. Tears spilled from my eyes, all of us in the room together to hear this grand announcement. My father was everything a husband should be. But it wasn't enough. Silence ruled my brother. My mother offered no explanation. I suppose her selfish desires were to serve as a solid explanation for the horrid ripping sound one only heard when every member if his family were being broken. Somehow, we knew, no matter how much my father was adamant about it being okay, we knew things would never be the same, so much damage by one person. As in war, the desires of one could turn a nation. This set the precedent for struggles to come. My brother's grades plummeted in school. Little did we know that the winds of change were to erupt upon us as like a tsunami, leaving all of us to drown.

My father may have been happy we missed the draft for Vietnam but no one saw this coming. Immediately we were sent to the front lines for the battle of our lives. My mother remarried. This man redefined abuse in the most horrid ways. He was an ex-military man twelve years my mother's junior. He had never been in war, never had children, He was married at least two other times. We couldn't tell our dad what was going on. He would go to war with this imposter and kill him. This jerk was violent and made promises of pain if we told anyone about the abuse. We knew those threats were not empty. We tried to concentrate on seeing dad when we could. We began immersing ourselves in schoolwork and building more model airplanes to help block out the violence in our house.

The new rules under this dictator of a man were suffocating. We were entering the teen years and still had a bed curfew of seven o' clock. Even when prom was in season, neither my brother nor I could attend. The curfew was not negotiable. Building model airplanes was our only escape.

We managed an escape, my brother and I. We were able to leave my mother's house and live with our grandmother. She protected us and defended us, things my mother never did. She would let no one hurt us anymore. My grandmother tried so hard to show my mother she deserved better. But no amount of talking could convince her to leave that abusive man. My mother stayed and endured the abuse for the rest of her life. This was one of my most poignant lessons in codependency.

My love for airplanes increased as I grew older, with my anger fanning the flames. I channeled all my angst into this process. I loved to read about them, loved to look at pictures of them; loved to dream of being an airline pilot someday. My hockey days were long over with. This was all I had left. Both hockey and flying represented a certain freedom. Skating on ice or flying in space made me free.

Now, you may be asking yourself, "Did any of these young man's dreams come true?"

No, they absolutely did not! I was meant for other things.

Now, it is Friday and as usual as an "alleged adult now" I celebrated the end of the week by flying down the banister of my house. As I slid down the banister past my scowling wife, disapproving of my definition of an exit, I did not realize the anguish that awaited me.

She said to me, "I don't have three children I have four", as I whizzed past her.

I kissed her quickly on the cheek and ran out to my car, telling her to have a good day. As I drove to work I noticed that the bright sunshiny day slowly turned to overcast. I eventually pulled up to the mental health clinic where I worked. As I entered I was met by two plainclothes detectives. They were both in dark suits and one looking more serious than the other.

The serious one showed me his badge and said, "Are you Dr. Thomas Shull?"

To which I replied in shock, "Yes, can I ask what this is about?"

The less serious looking one turned and said, "We want to talk to you about fraudulent practices."

I was aghast! I replied, in shock again, "What!"

This is my story. I am Dr. Tom Shull, AKA Dr. Tom as my patients call me. I was voluntarily going down to the police station. Thank goodness I was not under arrest. The detectives took me to a room and explained that several of my counselors that worked in the practice I owned filed complaints with the law against me. For the first time, I was informed my counselors felt I did not pay them what they were promised. I promised, per my contract with them, that they would earn seventy percent and I would only get thirty percent. The thirty percent would go for operating expenses and to take them out for lunches, or buy them gas cards or give them office birthday parties. I was shocked to say the least at what they did. They did have a ring leader, and she was ruthless. They were walking their captain to the plank unjustly. I asked if I could call my wife as she also managed the finances for the business. They told her to bring all the books down and they had their accountant go over everything with a fine tooth comb. After several grueling hours I was exonerated as everything was in place. They let me go. I was in shock. How could people who I gave everything I had stab me in the back? Of course their grueling ring leader was more professional in stirring the drama than she was at her actual paying job. When I hired them, none of them were currently employed. I took a risk on them when I should've cleaned house, burned the building and started from ground zero. The story of God flooding the Earth to start over with the human population suddenly became much more relatable.

My ruthless accuser quite in a rage, of course. She saved me the trouble. I was going to fire her anyway. Finally, a slight reprieve in the recent uproar settled over the place. I told the staff that they did not understand how insurances companies pay in private practice.

"They do not pay what you are worth or what we bill out," I told them.

They do not pay the next day either. Many of the counselors had never worked a private practice and no clue of its' inner workings. They were easily swayed by a strong-willed woman who "thought" she knew how insurance companies worked, manipulating the other's ignorance of the financial side of the mental health field. There was a deepening mysterious agenda. This is mental health where people are supposed to acquire tools to maintain a sound mind. But all the crazies were coming out of the woodwork.

One counselor, I found out later, reported me not only to the law, but The State Psychology Board as well. They investigated the insurance companies but found no fraud issues with the way I billed or paid my employees. Just a few months went by and I thought all is good in the land of OZ again. I tried to forgive and forget. Wrong again, this time it was Armageddon, and the war of the ages was on my home front.

This time everything that could possibly have gone wrong went wrong. I got a call from my attorney who said he was contacted by The State Psychology Board.

He explained with a serene affect, "It appears you will have to answer more fraud issues this time about a client."

"I cannot win", I told him.

I got an "official" letter soon after from the great State Board requesting my presence at an "inquiry."

My lawyer told me to come down to his office and discuss how all of this turmoil took form. I did exactly as my lawyer told me to do. He inquired about my back story and the reason why I went into the mental health field. He asked me the location of my office and what clients I counseled. He wanted to know it all because The Board already had all the information and he couldn't be left in the dark. He did not know what they would even accuse me, what they would throw at me. Neither did I, until they went full force and began taking actions in their legal proceedings. I learned much later that this Psychology Board was well hated and feared. This process was not rehabilitative but purely punitive, and sanctions were permanent

Mental health is crucial and is also the last form of treatment to be considered. My experiences growing up inspired to help others. If my mother had the help she needed growing up, the possibilities were endless as to how things in my family could have been different.

My career however started with a girl named Jan. I met this blue-eyed, blond-haired woman in college. She was a perfect example of any man's fantasies. Now, you'll have to realize that I considered myself homely, awkward and openly lacking in any form of confidence when it came to the opposite sex. I almost fainted when she sat down next to me in our college classroom and turned her blue eyes toward me and said that traumatizing word to me.

"HI!" Being the shy goof that I was, she had to repeat the word hi to me. She continued with, "Do you speak, or are you a mute?"

I thought, *"I'm a mutant,"* but I forcefully said, "No."

In reply, she quizzically retorted, "No, you don't speak?"

Then she giggled, because I had, in fact, said no. This was the beginning of what I thought could be a life-changing relationship for me. As you can probably imagine, the relationship would eventually crash and burn, like my career. This is the norm for me. Jan actually had experience with dating. I did not! Dating to me was more complicated than "particle theory" in physics. I grew up with brothers. My experience with girls was pretty much non-existent. When Jan would come close to me, or look at me, I trembled with fear and embarrassment. As our relationship as friends progressed, Jan would declare that her major was going to be psychology.

Impulsively, because my heart by now was in A-fib, beating through my chest, I blurted out, "Mine too!"

She smiled and I thought to myself, *"What did I just do? What's psychology? Did I just say that? Why would I say that?"* Later that day, Jan asked me for my phone number and I gave her every number I could think of so that she could reach me anywhere, anytime. I think at this point, my future career was taking second place to this blue-eyed, blond-haired beauty. I did not care what my career choice was or what the heck I would major in. I was in love.

The home telephone rang a few days later. Thinking it could be Jan calling, I became extremely excited and flew across the room in an effort to grab the phone out of my brother's hand, crashing into the table only to find out it wasn't even

Jan, but our Aunt Helen. I literally destroyed my face in the process. My brother calmly walked over to my broken body to retrieve the phone from my now dead hand. When I went to the doctors for my self-imposed injuries, the physician merely laughed.

Then I remembered my brother walking away, he mumbled idiot and said with a stern face, "Try not to get blood on Mom's new carpet."

So much for empathy! When Jan finally did call a few days later, she invited me out. It took me awhile to answer her because my jaw was wired shut from the acrobatic maneuvers earlier in the week. I am sure that Jan thought I was again suffering from some kind of selective mutism.

The day arrived for my big date with Jan. I pulled up to her house in my unimpressive 1974 pea green, AMC Gremlin minus the muffler. It had fallen off in route to her house a few blocks earlier. I had to get out of the car to throw the muffler into the trunk. The car was so loud! Thank god she did not seem to mind. If she did, she didn't show her irritation. I took her to dinner and a movie. When I dropped her off at home, she asked me if I wanted to kiss her. Of course, I froze. I was in a catatonic state. I had manifested instant catatonic state. Remember, I had never kissed a girl and had never had this type of closeness with a girl. I do remember being licked once by a dog in the face! But explaining my lack of experience with the dog story probably would've been a horrible idea. I wondered if that was the same feeling. That was it, a dinner, a movie ...always just dinner and a movie! Yea, I was definitely creative, and exciting to be with.

When I saw Jan after that incident, she asked me "What makes you so special?"

"I don't know myself," I replied. Looking back, this signaled a downward spiral in our relationship. I did not kiss her because intense fear caused a plethora of perspiration, but how was she to know, especially at my age as a college student, that I would be this shy? I loved girls, but lacked the courage. I never told her that I had no experience. How would I even begin to explain that? I continued to try and grow our relationship by bringing her flowers, candy, and a weird kaleidoscope lamp on Valentine's Day. Again, she said nothing about me not kissing her. Eventually, she would come to ask me if I was gay, to which I humorously replied, "No," but I'm generally happy as a rule. I thought my answer to her question was funny, but she didn't smile. She was not getting it, and I certainly did not get it. She did not understand that she needed to take the lead with this dorky guy. I certainly was not like her other dates---they were normal.

Several days later, she told me her father, a physician, had called her a tramp.

She asked me if I thought she was. Of course, I didn't really know how to respond to this question, so, in my usual, inexperienced and stupid manner, I responded with a joke.

"I have no empirical data to support such a conclusion," I said to her, and smiled as I said it.

Apparently, this was not the answer she was looking for. She retorted with an expletive and slammed my car door so hard that the handle of my Gremlin came off. She ran into her house, taking my door handle with her, looking back and scowling at me.

I thought to myself as she ran off, *"Did I say something wrong? Can I have my door handle back?"*

A week went by, and then a month went by. I didn't hear from Jan. I called her, but to no avail. Eventually, we concluded our class and I didn't take any more classes with her. I finally saw her in the atrium at school. I apologized for our last date and anything I might have said to offend her. What a relief it was to me when I saw her smile. She decided to give me another chance!

I decided to consult my worldlier friend who was experienced with women. He was a self-proclaimed expert in the "psycho dynamics" of the female species. I listened to this grand master as he imparted his wisdom to me in question form.

He said as he turned to me astonishingly, "You haven't kissed her yet, you idiot."

OK, now both my brother and my friend thought I was an idiot. Maybe I was. If seven people, in my case two, call you a horse, you had better get a saddle.

I said to my friend with reassurance, "I promise I will kiss her next time I see her."

To which he hesitatingly replied, "I hope it's not too late."

At the time, I wondered what the self-exalted mentor meant by that cryptic message. I would soon find out on my next date with Jan.

My next date was my last date with Jan. Since my Gremlin, my valiant steed, was being repaired with a new floor board. My mother accidentally put her foot through the rusted bottom. I got a new door handle and I had borrowed my father's Lincoln Continental. I bought $100 worth of roses with my $2.00 per hour job. In those days, things were cheaper, like my pay. It was my desire to present these beautiful roses to Jan with our first kiss now that I had this newfound courage instilled upon me by the wizard of romance. He, by the way, did not have a girlfriend at the time himself. I put my best jeans on, Kmart specials. I opened my shirt to reveal the few paltry hairs on my chest and went forth courageously into battle. I presented her with the roses as she smiled and thanked me. I jumped out of the car, opened and closed the door for her.

I made sure her seatbelt was fastened. After all, I was very safety conscious. The last thing I needed was for her to fly through a windshield on my watch. This was all done within a 30 second period. Then I took a huge breath and kissed her. *I've stunned her,* I thought. She looked so surprised. *I'm in baby, I'm in. She's mine.* She said nothing and was apparently in a coma. Again, I thought, the power of my kiss is terrifying. *Right.*

Jan remained silent as we drove to our usual dinner and a movie. Generally, she was a talking machine.

What gives? I saw another guy in a tender moment during the movie reach for the girl's hand. *That's probably what I'm supposed to do*, I thought. Of course, I reached for Jan's hand.

She immediately withdrew her hand and put it in her pocket stating, "My hand is just too cold."

I didn't think to ask any questions on what had just happened. When I finally drove her home in Dad's big Lincoln, she leaped out of the car faster than a beaver in heat, assuming there are horny beavers out there. I asked her politely if I could kiss her again.

She replied with an unmistakable and resounding "NO!"

My heated embarrassment made my face melt off my head followed by my heart. I wasn't sure what she said and I asked her to repeat it.

She said it again with determination this time. "NO!" "Don't look so sad, we can still be friends," she told me.

This is the death word to the male species. She then ran into the house closing the door behind her. As it started to rain, I turned to pick my dignity and facial parts off the sidewalk.

As I walked to the car in the dark, I saw a cat resting on the hood. It was a very black cat and I failed to see the distinct white line running down its back. I tried scooting the cat off the hood and it tried to piss on me. You'll never guess what I discovered next! It was not a cat! Wasn't this a perfect ending to a perfect day? I got pissed on times two. I went home smelling like I felt. I did not know what happened.

My mentor's words came back to me like a dream driving home. "I hope it's not too late!" I finally realized what he meant by his statement and it apparently was too late. Suddenly and as if prophetic or written in tarot cards, Billy Joel's "Tell Her About It" played on the radio and I found myself "Alone Again, Naturally".

I consulted with Mr. Wizard with regard to feminine issues again a few days later. He told me that it seemed I waited too long and she had probably been dating someone else behind my back. If only I had heard his wise words before! He exclaimed the rules of dating and the psychology of girls.

He calmly stated, "They expect guys to do the work, ask them out, make the first move, etc. If they like you, they go with you; if they don't, you're toast. She must have liked you."

He went on to explain, "Because she went out with you for a while, and only God knows why. Girls won't tell you what you should do, since you're an idiot."

Apparently, we established this already.

"She sent you behavioral"- (here is the psychology part) - "cues that you missed, my young Jedi."

I thanked Obi Won and walked away slowly into the sunset broken-hearted. I definitely learned from my mistakes and would not repeat them in the future. I'll take a girl miniature golfing, dancing or horseback riding, shark hunting, trying to find Bigfoot, anything that she wants next time instead of just a movie. Jan never called me again. There's no surprise there. We never contacted each other again. She never explained to me what had happened or why she rejected me. I figured girls do not do this either. My only guess was she felt I did not love her and only wanted her as a friend. This was not the reality though. My loss was due to my inexperience with the opposite sex. My lot was clear in life as Jan unknowingly set my career path in motion. I was probably destined to be a virgin monk with a psychology degree. I think about her now and then, realizing I may have lost the girl, but gained a psychology degree; a stepping stone into unemployment. With my new-found psychology degree I was able to pump gas, make pizzas, work construction and bring in shopping carts from a snow-plowed parking lot. Great clinical experience! I discerned one thing; however, working with the general public sucked. They define you and treat you according to your position or status, generally speaking. Along the way, I learned a bit of humility and decided to treat others as I would like to be treated.

An old Chinese saying I once came upon stated "To know others is considered knowledge; to know oneself is considered wisdom."

Pursuing psychology as a career focused on the wisdom part and on learning to not take myself too seriously. It is when we truly understand ourselves that we can begin to understand others, realizing that our deepest hurts and pains reflect our most genuine fears. I believe now that people require guidance, support, and love and above all: understanding. I had read Mother Theresa's poem "Anyway" and it made complete sense to me. My journey into psychology was a journey into self-discovery and self-growth. It was a humbling experience.

Since I wasn't doing very well on the sidewalk with my sunglasses, tin cup and little monkey, I attended graduate school taking as many classes as my measly paycheck permitted. My monkey did better than I did because eventually, a pretty girl came by and took him home with her. As he thumbed his nose at me driving off with her, I realized I had to go on for a master's degree if I would be of any use in life. I would not be upstaged by a chimp. I attended a State school and subsidized my income by teaching undergraduate students concepts of psychology that took me four years to grasp myself. Since I needed a better car, I also conducted intakes at a mental health center. Finally, I bought a better car, an Escort, which also broke down.

One of my internships while in graduate school was at a public mental health center. I was able to see human pain in its full form – indigent people with little or no food, shelter or means. Some had not taken a bath for weeks, had open sores on their bodies, or were completely delusional and were suicidal or severely depressed. My heart broke for these people. I think some may have been graduate psychology students. Two very seasoned psychologists with a keen sense of twisted humor supervised me while at the public mental health center.

Brimming with excitement with my first case, a good-looking young woman in a short skirt was waiting for me in the office. She was pretty, in great shape and was dressed rather well. She had an air of confidence and looked out place in contrast with the others in the facility. As I greeted the young lady, I heard a psychiatrist snickering outside my door as he discussed my new case with one of my supervisors. I ignored the banter and continued "single-minded" in my task to "cure" everyone who came through my door. Proceeding with the intake screening, something wasn't right. I couldn't put my finger on it. About half-way through the interview, my client disclosed that she was actually a man who was half-way through a sex change operation and was struggling with some depressive issues; hence the giggles from my supervisory staff outside my door. This "lady" did not return to the center as a result.

An envious student came up to me later and said in amazement, "How do you end up with the hot patients?"

"Well," I told him, "I was just lucky, I guess."

A sociopathic disheveled man with a dingy jacket and mean look was my next patient. He showed me two "pockmarks" on his body.

"That's where they got me," he told me when I asked him what they were.

"Who got you?" I asked him in a surprised manner.

He said he had shot it out with police and took two bullet holes. He was frustrated because he did not hit any officers.

"Oh…" I replied.

Just another routine day in mental health! I then asked Snake Pliskin if he was "packing heat." He told me no, because I would have been dead already. With this, I excused myself from the room and went to the bathroom to throw-up. But the formerly white walls and toilet seat has been peed on by that sociopathic disheveled man. My supervisor told me to get back in there, after I clean the toilet. Redirecting my graduate degree to French studies sounded fantastic right about now.

Another case at this center involved a very depressed young man who claimed a conversion disorder: anxiety symptoms placed in the body creating a pseudo physiological condition like hysterical blindness; where no genuine medical condition exists via medical testing. This situation wasn't as complicated as that definition though. He reported neck pain and being unable to move his neck. During this treatment session, a new counselor came in. Although tears welled up in my eyes, I managed to hide it from her. She was a quadriplegic moving around in her wheelchair, talking by means of a little stick near her mouth. Getting nowhere in therapy with my depressed guy with the cervical pain, a brainstorm suddenly hit me: I would transfer him to her.

One session with her and his neck was miraculously better. In fact, he virtually cart-wheeled out of her office telling us, I'm cured, I'm cured.

The client left her office exclaiming "She's really good!"

I asked her later what she said to him.

"I didn't say a word. He just said, 'I'm better, thanks'. He turned his head toward the door, got up and left." she told me rather surprised.

"He was right," I told her laughing with a red face, "You are really good!"

We both laughed and remained good friends throughout my tenure there.

Later that week, a homeless man came in to tell me his sad story of woe. I instantly felt my heartstrings being yanked to the point of snapping. Of course, I gave him my last $5.00 for something to eat. Well, little did I know he drank his lunch and my supervisor thanked me for enabling him! How do you spell sucker?

"Before you jump to conclusions about people, know your facts," my supervisor counseled. I asked him to pull the sign off my butt that says "kick me". Working in mental health is so much fun.

When I finally graduated with my master's degree in Counseling Psychology, I felt I was all that and a bag of chips. In reality, I was just beginning to understand myself, human behavior and the world in general. I applied for a position teaching general psychology and abnormal psychology classes at a community college. During the interview, I was asked, of course, about my past experience. When I told the school I had no teaching experience, I was told neither do the students. They threw a text at me, literally, and told me to create a course outline and develop some tests. I was told if I could do that, I'm hired. I did, and I was!

My first day was horrifying. I just stood there and looked at the class. They looked at me like I was an insect in a glass jar. This seemed like hours.

Ten minutes must have gone by before one courageous student spoke up to say, "Are you going to teach us something or just stand there?"

I said I hadn't decided yet and the class laughed. The ice was broken. I taught strictly from the book that first term and was fairly serious, but as time progressed, I began to feel more comfortable and loosened up a bit. Still covering the book, I added interactive "doing" exercises and material I stole from The Tonight Show to make classes more fun. The class became a popular class and students wanted in the now overbooked classes. I guess I made learning fun, which I discovered later was an act of treason and heresy in the academic world. A full-time professor ratted me out, so to speak, to the tribunal – the hierarchy. I was called before the Dean of Students.

"Academics," I was told, "is a very serious matter."

The dean said that she could not have an instructor mocking higher learning.

After all, "young minds are very impressionable."

Several of my students staved off my execution by writing to the Dean commending my teaching techniques. Given the fact that many students wanted in my classes, they pointed out, just further supported how good an instructor they felt I was. The solid academic scores supported my teaching methods.

Dressing up like a student in jeans, tennis shoes and a plaid shirt on the first day of class of my last semester teaching, I thought I would show my new students how prejudice can influence behavior. I walked in the classroom and sat down with the kids. Not being much older than them myself, I turned to a student and said, "Hey, have you heard anything about this professor?"

She replied with serious focus, "No, have you?"

I retorted, "He's a son of a gun, incredibly hard, grades on a "C" curve and is downright rude to his students."

She replied in horror, "Are you sure? I heard he was awesome; that's about all."

Another male student overheard us with a concerned look on his face and said, "He's an asshole, right?"

"Right," I told him, a complete one.

Another kid looked me directly in the eye and said, "Then why are you here?"

He exhibited some deductive logic and I put him in his place. "Because all I need is this last class and I graduate," I said, "so I'm willing to tough it out."

Almost the entire class was in mutiny mode now – group-think at its finest! Several kids wanted to leave the class right then and sign up for a new instructor.

To make matters worse, I blurted out, "Look!" very loudly, "he's even late" and everyone looked at the clock on the wall.

Finally I got up, closed the door and said to the class, "What should we do guys?"

Several students discussed leaving the class and taking the class with a different instructor. Others wanted to tough it out like me, while others sat quietly confused not knowing what the heck to do. One kid sat quietly in the back playing with a miniature guillotine. I always wondered about him.

Then I laughed out loud, went to the podium and said, "I'm your instructor, so what have we learned?"

To which one fearful student replied, "Get away from the podium you idiot before he comes in and you get in trouble."

This trick almost backfired until I showed the class my I.D. card and then you could have heard a pin drop. I laughed, then the students laughed and again I asked "What did we learn?"

We processed "group think" that day and loss of identity ... mine. I told them that what you hear or see may not always be reality. Perceptions are not always reality. Do your own research. My last semester teaching was a hit and I personally felt more empowered having impacted on my students in a safe, educative environment.

I then ran into a student from my last class, after the term, at K-mart where I again was buying my K-mart special jeans. She stated that she had become a more independent and "aware" person because of that one exercise years ago. They say that if you reach at least one kid, then it was all worthwhile. Apparently I did!

I finally went on to teach a year of advanced abnormal psychology in a graduate school at a university. While doing that, I also worked as a placement director in a workshop for the developmentally handicapped. I could barely find employment for myself, yet was handed the seemingly impossible task of helping the developmentally disabled find employment in the community. The neuropsychologist there must have seen something in me, or felt sorry for me, because I only found about three people jobs. This doctor took me under her wing and stated that her husband was president of a school of professional psychology and she encouraged me to apply to the doctoral program in clinical and neuropsychology. I was stunned. Doctoral programs were very hard to get into and I barely made my master's degree.

"This is well out of my league" I told her:

You can't take a sow's ear and make it into a silk purse.

She told me to apply.

LEARNING TO FLY

CHAPTER TWO

There was a combination of three things to earn my acceptance to the doctoral program at a School of Professional Psychology: (1) the president's wife gave me a personal recommendation; (2) my grade point average in my master's program was a 4.0 straight A average; and (3) I did well on a graduate level competency examination.

The president's wife was a wonderful and practiced lady. She was tall, but tough-looking, no-nonsense individual, with broad shoulders and a wry look to match. She saw my potential, something I never thought I had. She felt I had a gift for people. The program was intensive, but as I practiced later on, I realized it was some of the finest training I had ever received.

Her words came back to me while I was working on my dissertation: "This is the bottom drawer to my cabinet. Every week I want to see progress on your dissertation. It better be there or I'm done with you."

Believing in me as she did, I wasn't about to let her down. I added to my dissertation daily, leaving it in that drawer for her to read. She was an incredible neuropsychologist. I learned so much about brain pathology from her, despite her drill instructor mentality.

Schools of psychology teach psychology. What they don't teach is how to survive as a psychologist in the real world. I quickly realized how little I knew about human behavior and treatment issues with only a master's degree in psychology. At the master's level I had been given strategies, techniques, etc. But, the fundamental skills only develop with on-the-job-training.

"It probably took several years for a person to become mentally ill, so anything you do probably can't hurt so much" my professor reasoned.

At this point, all I can think is thank goodness, because on the path to learning, I am sure there's many bodies left devastated along the way.

I'm convinced that people who enter the mental health field either absolutely love the behavioral sciences or secretly want to find out more about themselves and their own problems without facing the possible stigma of psychotherapy. Case in point- one of my fellow students whom I felt an odd kinship with, had a strange habit of opening the large side window of our classroom during lunch hour, (our classes were 8 hours per day), and sitting on the ledge. The thing that increased my autonomic nervous system was the fact we were 50 stories above the ground. She fed the pigeons. I slowly approached her asking if she would do me a personal favor and come back in the classroom.

She looked at me, laughed and sarcastically replied, "You worry too much; I'm fine."

I prayed we wouldn't get high winds that day. She later moved on to another school to obtain her doctoral degree; probably a school with a higher building.

Most of the Doctoral instructors and professors were well-loved. However, many of them had their quirks. You had to figure out what they wanted just to survive. This is a phenomenon all students in all schools eventually realize. One instructor taught in a nightshirt on the evening weekend courses. An 88 year old visiting professor who held both a PhD and MD degree fell asleep during the lecture. We didn't have the heart to wake him, so we ordered pizza. When he did wake up, we fed him. Although we all passed his course, I'm not sure how much we learned. I think he probably was returned to the nursing home again.

I never studied so hard in my life! At 32 years old, I was told I aged badly. Intent to learn everything I could, I over-studied, however, with teachers who had worked with "the greats" in the field; Dr. Carl Rogers, Dr. Abraham Maslow, Dr. Rudolph Dreikurs, to mention a few. One day I decided to screw with the minds of my fellow classmates. I basically spit in their soup, so to speak. In a group therapy class, we all sat in our usual seats. One day, I sat in "someone else's" seat. This person (future psychologist) got angry and lashed out at me that I took his seat. My professor winked at me and he sat back to enjoy the performance. Drama at its finest erupted! Soon the whole class (group think) defended him. How could I not respect the other student? Who did I think I was? These were the war cries, "Kill, kill, kill,"

Someone shouted, "Throw Tom out of the 50th floor, but move the other student on the ledge first."

My professor finally intervened. Remember, these are future psychologists.

He stated smiling, "I admire Tom's courage. He disrupted your comfortable world and he was able to touch your inner insecurities."

Everyone sat and listened except the one kid whose chair I took. Three weeks later, he pulled the chair out from under me; "by accident," he said. This foreshadowed more of this type of behavior to reveal itself in my professional future. I discovered that the mental health field is not always healthy and at times, even dangerous, almost an oxymoron. It can be downright abusive to patients, students and colleagues. Prior to deinstitutionalization back in the 1970's, it must have been horrible. Doctors probably conducted pre-frontal lobotomies and shock treatments (ECT) to "zombify" patients in some instances and put them under behavioral control, hence the term lobotomized.

One day I left for home with a female student. She appreciated riding the train together after class since it was late at night. I had to leave one stop before her; however, and as I said goodbye, a man in a trench coat got on board. I saw she felt uneasy, I told her I would stay on. She said no she would be fine. I told her to move to a full car, and I'd see her in the morning. I did not want to leave her but she insisted. I worried about her that night. The next day, I saw her and was relieved. I asked her if she made it home ok. She told me that the guy who came on board flashed her when her stop came.

"I laughed and told him I'd seen bigger" she said coyly.

Then she shot his little bugger with a squirt gun she had hidden in her pocket.

"You should have seen how red his face got," she stated laughing.

Now this is a gusty lady, I thought, but cautioned her.

She told me, "You worry too much."

I found out later her sister was the ledge sitter, go figure.

The snow was blowing very hard on the night class ended at 11:00 p.m. As we began our individual trips home, the streets were vacant. Though we knew our professor was very anal, I could not believe he hadn't cancelled class that night. Making my way towards the train, I felt like I was being watched. I looked around frantically but couldn't spot anyone through the snowy darkness. I cursed my professor for putting me in this situation. Hopefully someone stole all the wheels on his Toyota Corolla and he'd have to walk to the train station too. I found out later, he was dating a student-go figure. I'll bet she didn't have to walk to the train station. A few minutes went by, and I spotted a tall hooded figure darting in and out of shadows between buildings on the streets. I was right!

I was being followed, probably by a disgruntled psychology doctoral student out for revenge. As I proceeded down the street, I looked back and saw no one. I figured I'd been studying psychology too long, because now I'm paranoid and delusional. I rounded a building and I could see the train station just ahead. I ducked in between the crevasse of two buildings and waited, determined to figure out if I was being followed, or just losing my mind. Suddenly this dark figure passed the crevasse, looked left and right, carrying a silver object that I took for a knife in his left hand. Maybe this was a very shiny spoon. Maybe he was lost and couldn't find the soup kitchen.

He moved forward, jockeying to the left of the building. I darted out quietly toward the station looking back. I saw him suddenly look at me entering the train and then disappear into an alley. I didn't realize why he ducked into an alley until I turned around and saw a policeman come out the train station doors. I breathed a sigh of relief thanking God for the boys in blue. I went through the door of the train and thanked the policeman for his service. I wanted to tell the officer about the creep following me but I looked through the windows for the hooded figure and he disappeared, again. I couldn't waste the officer's time with an invisible assailant. I kept repeating to myself, "I'm not delusional, I'm not delusional."

I told my mother later what transpired and she told me, "It was your guardian angel in blue."

My wife agreed I was indeed delusional. That's what wives are for, to give you a reality check.

I can't blame my wife for questioning me on what I saw. The first time I met my wife, I literally bumped into her at my optometrist's office. We are both acutely myopic, like two bespectacled turtles. Thank goodness, she never really got a good look at my face at the time; she would have run in terror. Nevertheless she has been the best thing in my life. I did not repeat my past errors regarding dating. It worked! I finally got the girl. She helped me tell my story. Both my dad and wife strongly encouraged the writing of this book even though I trashed it at least three times in the seven years I have been writing it. It collected more dust than my file cabinets. My old microbiology teacher would have a field day with the new organisms that grew on it.

I moved on to my pre-doctoral internship. I also decided to enter psychotherapy myself for a few months for two reasons: (1) to find out what it is like for me; after all, I'd be doing this to others, and (2) I was stressed. Therapy went well and I learned ways to effectively de-stress myself. I learned more about myself, and how positive thinking and self-confidence can accomplish almost anything, like finishing graduate school. I finished with a 3.9 average! Not too bad for someone labeled an "idiot" by friends and family (brother). I finished this stressful chapter of my life! Now off to new adventures.

I went on to my pre-doctoral internship where an addictions counselor thought Sigmund Freud was addicted to mainlining heroin. I tried to correct him, but he said, "Oh kid, you've got a lot to learn." Everyone knows it was cocaine. I learned a lot about addictions. I also worked in an adolescent recovery group and learned about cow tipping from drunken youths. How fun is that? The kids liked me and told me all their secrets on how they fool the staff. I worked hard to gain their trust. I eventually got them to see they were the ones fooling themselves. I left feeling I accomplished something. The fact that those kids remained abstinent while I was there was the highlight of my experience, and I learned that you cannot really tip a cow.

ARMAGEDDON

CHAPTER THREE

Samantha was a pre-doctoral intern, four years in. She was a self-declared "senior intern" because she had been there so long. She seemed genuinely nice. I liked her. As did others, I discovered later that Sam was Dr. Jekyll and Mrs. Hyde. This mercurial individual targeted me for destruction for some unidentified reason unexplained even today.

Sam persuaded the nursing staff to spy on me, taking notes on my coming and going, noting any concerns they had about me. On our last day, she forwarded copies of her spy notes to the school and the hospital administration. I was basically screwed. The crux of it was that I always treated her with kindness, so I couldn't understand why she considered me the Anti-Christ. She micro-managed those interns who were not from her school acting like a dictator, blatantly favoring those that were from her school.

Cal, a neuropsychology intern, laughed and thought it was funny, until she took her cruel type of sarcasm out on him one day. We took a pool to hire a hit man or woman. We were equal opportunity employers, but we came up short. All kidding aside, my goal was to sidestep Sam at all costs, not talk with her, laying low until I graduated. This was impossible. She criticized me for not being able to urinate under 30 seconds when I used the bathroom. Our illustrious supervisor was rarely at the sight supervising us. Other interns felt he was golfing or attending to his practice. When a young attractive master's level female student came to be supervised and found him not there, he left me a note stipulating me to supervise her. Then who would supervise me? Sam? She was out to crucify me and throw my Clorox-bleached bones to the dogs.

I tried to talk to the school about Sam's favoritism amongst interns.

The Dean of Students stated calmly, "Let's just hope you graduate!"

"Thanks for the support!" Was all I had to say?

I was righteously pissed off. I wasn't going to lift the toilet seat or clean it either. Sam complained that I took extra time at lunch, was working at my doctoral dissertation at the site. My school allowed this and contracted with the site for this privilege as we were doing a study at this hospital too. I was supposedly spending more than 45 minutes with patients, was using too much humor and toilet paper (a cardinal sin), seemed to be cavalier about things, didn't adhere to her rules, thought cow poop would make good alternative fuel source, didn't like frosted flakes, and adding insult to her injury, drove a Ford Escort, which she despised. I was a dead man walking.

While fending off what Cal called "my nemesis," I endured additional abuse from the master's degree level counselor named Craig. He was so insanely jealous that he pitched fruit at me while I walked down the hall, pulled a chair out from under me while I was preparing to sit in a group therapy session, and told me he absolutely would not obtain a doctoral education because it was a useless degree. He maintained he personally had just as much knowledge about human behavior and psychology as one who held a doctoral education. I told Craig he was right, getting a doctoral education would not be of any use to him at all. He agreed immediately. I rolled my eyes. He took any moment to put me down in front of staff. He and Sam were the perfect satanic couple. In psychology, they call this folie a deux; shared psychosis. I had more respect for the patients because they knew they had mental health issues and wanted help, unlike the staff, who didn't. Complaints to the school fell on deaf ears. I was told to "do whatever you have to do and survive." At this point, I felt that they could mail my Ph.D. at the end of my internship to my family as I would have been Killed in Action (KIA) in the mental health field, or KBS (Killed by Sam).

Aside from fending off my "colleagues," I did have some interesting experiences at the site. I met a Canadian exchange doctoral student named Shawn who was actually fairly sane and had common sense; a rarity in the field it seemed. I bonded with him and him with me. He gave me tips on how to sidestep Craig and Sam to keep under the radar. He had a great sense of humor and recognized that the way to help others was to be supportive, loving, encouraging and to redirect and reframe negative thinking to positive thinking. We were kindred spirits and hung out when we could. He introduced me to a lovely young nurse called Kathy. She was one of two directors there. She was supportive and so caring. She was a veteran however at this hospital and could be no nonsense when needed. She didn't take crap from anyone, even psychiatrists. They respected her because she was direct, ethical and honorable. Being guys and all, Shawn and I also happened to notice, of course, that Kathy was very pretty, but in a drill sergeant way. She put Sam in her place on more than one occasion and was not concerned about what the hospital or Sam's school might think. I really liked Kathy. She always gave me a heads up when Sam was in the area, sort of like "shark alert" on a beach. She defended me at times, like a big sister, against Craig. She told him to back off or she would personally write him up. He was scarce when Kathy was around. Shawn and Kathy were like rays of sunshine in the dark abyss of a new age. When she was around I was like The BMOC (Big Man on Campus), when she was not I was dirt.

Trouble always seemed to find me at my internship. To the point where I thought I would eventually be forced to apply to the sanitation department next. Or throw myself out the window, providing I moved any student that was already on the ledge out of my way. During my first few weeks, I attended a group therapy session and a man in a suit sat next to me. He started to tell me a little bit about every member in the group, their diagnosis, and how the hospital was treating their illnesses. I took out a pen and pad, taking notes. This was a very learned doctor; probably a psychologist or psychiatrist. Perceptions are not always reality though. A nice-looking man with deep set eyes of blue then sat on my left and wore sandals, faded jeans and a white cardigan sweater. He pulled out a pipe and the "doctor" next to me in the suit reminded him he couldn't smoke in the group.

I said with a stern face, "Yeah, no smoking!"

I turned to the man in the suit and said, "So what's the gig?"

The man in the suit looked at me directly and stated, "What do you mean?"

I re-stated, "What's this guy's mental health diagnosis."

The man in the sweater laughed and said, "Young man, why don't you ask me."

I gasped thinking, *oh boy, he heard me.*

I turned and said politely, "Well, I was actually asking the doctor."

He replied with a smile, "I am the doctor, a psychiatrist who leads this after-care group and you are my student in this group."

I said jokingly, "That's funny. This guy looks like a doctor, he's in a suit; you're in jeans and sandals."

"Can you believe this guy?" I said to the man in the suit with amazement.

To which the man in the suit replied, "He's right, he is the doctor, I'm a patient. I'm schizophrenic and I cut off my penis six months ago." I was stunned to say the least.

Again, the jeans doctor laughed and said, "Never judge a book by its blue jeans young man."

Open mouth, insert foot!

It only got better after that. In another episode, Shawn and I were walking to the "closed psychiatric unit" where the more clinically impaired patients were housed. A man dressed casually and nicely with a briefcase called out to Shawn and me as we opened the door.

He said anxiously, "Hold the door, please, I'm a visitor and I'm leaving now."

So, we held the door open.

Shawn remarked, "Boy that guy is in a hurry, huh?"

Then after he hopped on an elevator, he hailed a cab and was gone in a flash. Sam ran down the hallway with a plethora of nurses shouting, "Good, bonehead!" at me.

Turns out Shawn and I inadvertently let out a patient who was probably now on his way to Portugal. I was screwed and Sam let the entire hospital know, including the Sanitation Department and hospital administration. I asked Kathy for cyanide. She stated that she could not do it as it would violate her ethical code and she needed her license.

She gave me a hug, smiled and said, "Don't worry hero, he'll be back tomorrow."

She was right … and he was! Apparently, he had cab fare for only three blocks. When the cab driver realized, he was an "escapee," he returned him to the hospital immediately. Shawn and I both breathed a sigh of relief. However, we were chided in front of other nurses and doctors by both Sam and Craig. I came out of the hallway looking desperate, disillusioned and depressed. I looked up and saw Kathy approaching, smiling, her hand up as if to give me a high five. I raised my hand and they both met in a thunderous clap. She looked back and winked at me as she walked by. She made my day and I have always thought of Kathy with a smile in my heart. She was a wonderfully encouraging friend and colleague, especially when I needed it most. Her bright reddish hair belied what was underneath, a quiet, sensitive and deeply caring nurse, whose compassion for others was contagious. She was my hero. To this day, I miss her.

I spied an acquaintance, a person I briefly worked with at a nursing home after finishing my Bachelor's Degree.

Our eyes met and we smiled simultaneously as I said, "Hey Joe."

"Hey Tom," came the response.

"What are you doing here?" I asked almost curiously.

It turns out his brother had an alcohol issue with some serious depressive episodes and he was here to be given an "intake," an introductory assessment. The intake was given to another intern to handle, but we talked about my times at this nursing home and laughed.

He said assertively and with a smile, "You were quite the card, but just what we needed. You just ruffled too many feathers."

I instantly knew what he was referring to and had a flashback of my experiences at this nursing home. I was at odds with Kerry, the young administrator who I worked for as an activity aid. I would follow the prescribed plan of activities, but put my own slant on things as usual. Apparently, Kerry had strict guidelines and anyone who violated those guidelines was subjected to summary discipline, which I took to mean summary execution. Kerry was short in appearance and sharply dressed. She had a pointed nose and a sharp manner to match.

I told Kerry the only way to get these older people into an activity like Bingo is to provide donuts and coffee, living things up. When I ordered donuts and coffee from the kitchen, provided mood lighting, a kaleidoscope of lights, dimmed the house lights and got a microphone out while jumping on a table belting out numbers, like a poor imitation of Ferris Bueller, I was summarily disciplined by Kerry. She told me I could not be Ferris Bueller anymore nor could I order donuts from the kitchen for the residents.

I said to her in a convincing tone, "Look at the turnout; everyone's out of their beds, even the terminally disillusioned,"

She was not amused. When I adhered to her policy of not using "food" as reinforcement, only the janitors showed up, and they didn't stay for Bingo. I loved entertaining these folks, listening to war stories or stories of the depression, or Model T Fords. So, I decided to be bold and roll the dice. I broke Kerry's rules and went for broke, which eventually left me broke. When I ordered donuts, cranked up "In the Mood," and jumped onto the table belting out Bingo numbers, then screaming out "winner at table two" like I was at the casino, I was back in trouble. We laughed; I got applause, and then glanced over to Joe who pointed to Kerry. She was yet again, not amused. I got applause and a pink slip. I turned in my microphone and nametag, said goodbye to a few residents. One of those residents was a B-17 bomber pilot whose stories of WWII I visualized many times.

I left quietly with one female staff and Joe looking at me saying, "While you lasted, you were lots of fun."

They smiled wishing me well. After reminiscing with Joe, I continued my way as a lowly intern. I think the cockroach I spied walking in the lounge area garnered more respect until he was squashed by Sam in her heels. She then gazed at me and smiled in a sardonic way. I empathized with the roach, but knew what she meant.

I tended to be somewhat of a Patch Adams, even though I did not know who he was at the time. I thought I must be possessed. I just did things that felt natural to me. I admit I was a bit of a rebel, but with a good cause. I gave a good luck card to a patient who had what was then called Multiple Personality Disorder. I wasn't sure which personality I was giving the card to, however, so I came back with three more cards. I received a watercolor picture back and a brief hug from this patient thanking me for the time I spent with her and the compassion. Of course, Sam would find out. I swear to this day she bugged the room I saw patients in. She reported it to the charge nurse who reported it to my supervisor in note form because she couldn't find him. My school was informed and I was told "I crossed my boundaries" by giving a patient, or in this case a group of patients in one body, get well and good luck cards. I also accepted a watercolor picture from her. Sam snickered; Craig laughed as I was admonished and Shawn and Kathy bought me a beer after work and told me not to take it personally.

Shawn said with humor, "Yeah they were abused as children."

We all laughed at that.

Later that week I met a sociopathic and paranoid motorcycle gang leader who hated people in general, but curiously enough liked me. He told me, "I hate people but like you." Again, go figure. I could talk him into complying with the activities on the unit. I could almost hear the song "Bad to the Bone" play as he strolled down the hallway! He made Arnold Schwarzenegger look like a minister. He was diagnosed with Bi-polar Disorder, amongst other things, and when I worked with him, he took his medicine and improved.

He asked me if there was anything he could do to thank me, so I said, "Well, there is this intern; her name is Sam. Maybe you could take her on a long bike ride?"

I was kidding … he was serious!

"Sure Doc, where is she?"

I sat stunned and said, "Thanks anyway," and delayed his exodus from the mental health center for just a while longer.

Everyone feared him except me. We were pals! Even Sam stayed away. I was like his little buddy while he was there.

I would say to people in my best Cuban slash Al Pacino accent, "Say hello to my big friend."

Even Craig backed off. I laughed all the way down the hallway *thinking yeah don't piss me off.*

One day I was conducting my rounds when a six or seven-year-old child ran past me down the hallway.

I turned rapidly and said, "Timmy, it's me, Tom. Slow down buddy, you're going to fall and get hurt."

He ran into the corner of the hallway and crunched up there.

I walked toward him saying calmly, "Why so scared?"

He pointed behind me, without uttering a word at first.

"Because of them," he nervously blurted out.

Without looking back, I said to him, "There's no one there Timmy; just me and you buddy."

He was literally shaking.

"Come with me, give me your hand. No one is here. No one will hurt you."

Again, he pointed. "Look, Tom, look."

I decided to humor him and started to turn around when I heard the charge nurse say, "Now Tom, move away, we know what to do. Learn from the situation."

With that, I was terrified to see the psychiatrist, charge nurse, two security guards and an aide ready to bring the wanted felon down. He hid behind me and they walked over ready to pounce.

I said, "You guys are scaring him."

They picked him up kicking and screaming and took him to a seclusion room. He was strapped down and medicated. Sam looked at me very disapproving and, of course, slyly wrote this down in her little journal. I was called on the carpet by the charge nurse for "interfering with professional staff," a misdemeanor, but nevertheless, an offense. The next day, I found Timmy got angry and uplifted his food and ran, bringing upon him the brut squad. I talked with him and eventually conducted some counseling with him and his family. He was eventually released from his Gulag. Sam scowled, Craig grimaced, and I was frozen.

I confronted an alcoholic lady one day who vehemently denied she was an alcoholic, despite her having 3 times the B.A.C. level over the legal limit.

When I told Kathy that this lady lied, Kathy said calmly, "Oh really!" and ruffled my hair with her hand.

Shawn laughed from the sideline and said laughingly, "You really are in your 4th year, right?"

Another time at this same facility, I stayed up with a very depressed patient and told her funny stories, which I think made her more depressed. I danced in the room with an 86-year-old patient to Begin the Beguine, making her laugh and think about her school days. She was a good dancer, despite my having two left feet.

On one occasion, Shawn and I witnessed a nurse get into a power-struggle with a depressed teen over having a privilege to listen to his radio, which was calming him.

She stated, "He couldn't have it until after dinner two hours from now," even though he was frustrated.

She was the law and she enforced the rules. Shawn looked at me and we were deciding whether to inform the nurse that it probably would be a good idea if he gets it now instead of after dinner because it calms him and he was already angry. It was too late, however, and he lunged at her as she continued to enforce "the law." Security was called; he was put on a gurney, tethered and given a shot. Somewhat leery of past problems, I decided discretion was the better part of valor. I was probably next to be tied to a gurney and medicated if I had said anything. Sam was still in charge. She would probably have insisted on a lobotomy as well or lethal injection ... her preferred method.

The following week, another patient would not take her medication. The nurse left frustrated.

She told me, "She's all yours kid."

I asked her what the problem was and the nurse exclaimed in a frustrated tone, "She refuses her meds, she's very manipulative."

I entered the diabolical chamber and there she sat ... "The Queen of Resistance!" looking sternly at me with a face only a mother could love.

"Hi," I said to her somewhat hesitatingly.

She replied, "What the hell do you want twerp?" I snapped back,

"I want to bargain. Are you up to it girl?"

"Say what?" She replied.

I repeated my statement.

"I'll stand on my head if you take your meds today," I replied.

She said, "How do I trust that you will stand on your head if I take my medication?"

I replied, "How do I trust you to take your meds if I stand on my head?"

She said thoughtfully, "Good point. OK, let's shake on it."

We shook hands and she replied, "My word is my bond."

As I stood on my head in the doorway, she said, "Well, I'll be darned. You really are a man of your word."

I said, "Fine, (while upside-down), now take your meds!"

She did, which pleased me and her physician. I saw a pair of feet clad in white shoes coming towards me while I was still upside down.

Then a familiar voice called out, "Quit playing around and get back to work."

It was the night charge nurse. She laughed as I righted myself. Thank God it wasn't Sam or Craig. I thanked the patient for living up to her bargain.

"Anytime, Doc," she said.

I gained an instant rapport and trust with this patient and worked with her until her release. Thereafter, she was always compliant with her medication, even if I had to stand on my head now and then. Who was conditioning who?

A difficult moment incurred when a patient with similar ethnic background as me was admitted to the closed unit, whom I will refer to as John. John only spoke in his native tongue, relying on me for interpretation. I was told he was a bright engineering student bent on self-destruction. Maybe he was interviewed by Sam or Craig? Why else would anyone want to consider suicide? I found John to be a very handsome, young, very intelligent individual who indeed during my interview with him, was hopelessly depressed. He was assessed very high potential for self-harm. This was serious now. After the interview, the nurse who headed up the closed unit (lockdown unit) said that this guy is "clinically bats," her new term for people who do not contact reality very well. I requested they isolate him from anything that could bring harm such as: combs; toothbrushes; shoestrings; Sam; Craig, etc. However, the psychiatrist assessed this young man who had a history of several suicidal attempts and declared he was calm and grounded enough to shave himself.

"Shave himself absolutely not" I shouted with disbelief.

They called the charge nurse who said quietly, "Be quiet."

Craig was there saying, "Shut up, you're an intern. Just learn and don't create problems." The nurse stated, "The psychiatrist assessed him to be safe and he is the final authority-not you." I'm thinking *something is really wrong here.*

I was incredulous! This was a candid camera episode and I started looking for the hidden camera. Where was Allen Funt? I called my school and asked for advice. I don't recall now who I talked to.

They told me to "keep my mouth shut and not to make any waves."

Two days later, I looked for John in his room, but only saw remnants of a spray of blood on the walls where he used to be. He could dislodge the blade from the razor and cut his wrists and throat. No one said a word to me afterward. I even walked off the unit in disbelief completely disillusioned. At this point, I wondered if it was too late to apply to ACME Trucking Company. The words mental health seemed like an oxymoron. I was incredulous with disbelief. I was angry. I never saw John again, never knew what happened to him. No one would talk about john.

Curiously enough after this event, I had earned respect from at least most of the staff. I found myself suddenly occasionally responsible for supervising a young master's level student. Unfortunately for her, she exhibited what I believe to have been common sense; a trait not well received on a psych unit. Like me, she was treated as rat excrement. So, I decided to take her under my wing. Also like me, she, was to be "supervised" by my supervisor, Casper the Ghost. When I tried to make this known to the school, they again told me to concentrate on getting through my internship with the least resistance possible. This was told to me by my ethics professor. I realized this was probably good advice, however, difficult to swallow with a conscience. We bonded as she "shadowed" me. She was aghast as well at the craziness she saw on the unit. I reminded her to stay focused on learning, to stay close to me and watch everything. I tried to give this younger, intelligent, morally good natured master's level individual, everything I had gained in my experiences and education. Meanwhile, however, I felt I was the black sheep of the Psychiatric Department. I felt they couldn't wait until my time was up. Honestly, neither could I. Tammy, the master's level intern and I, got along very well. She ran things by me constantly. She was a blond who had dark green eyes, always listening to the patients' needs. When my supervisor finally showed up for a guest appearance, she asked if it was okay that a doctoral intern supervised her.

He replied, "He's directly under me and remember, I'm actually still supervising both of you and will sign off on both of you."

Tammy and I looked at each other saying nothing. Remembering when I talked I was told to keep my mouth shut … I did!

A terminal cancer patient was having a difficult time coming to terms with grief and death. We took shifts attending to her and she seemed to appreciate this. Tammy and I wanted to lift her spirits, even if we couldn't cure her. I told my best jokes, even if they sucked, and she laughed. I would be holding her hand, crying quietly alone with her late at night together. She was gaunt, her eyes swollen. She looked very pale. We both cried together as she taught me how to be courageous, especially when facing death. Sam passed by the nurse's station and was told that I held a lady's hand while she cried. I crossed boundaries-again, and was called on the carpet for the millionth time. Tammy was so angry; she vowed to kill all hostages. I told her they would probably give her a lobotomy if she continued, so she dropped the idea. I felt I was being beaten up more than Rocky Balboa was. Cal, looking unshaven, smelly and disheveled as usual came upstairs to where I was.

He looked at me and said, "I think your nemesis is winding down her internship."

He then smiled and went quietly back to his labyrinth in the neuropsychological department in the bowels of the hospital. I felt a punch hit my left arm and thought, *now they're into physical violence.* Looking around, Kathy was there smiling.

"How are you holding up slugger?" she asked.

"I'm still here," I replied holding my breath.

"Well, that's a good thing. You're a survivor," she told me.

She informed me she had talked to Shawn and they were going out to dinner and they wanted Tammy, my new protégé and I, to go along as well. Tammy had plans with her boyfriend so I went solo. Kathy really encouraged me that night. She went on about how I was always there for them, taking extra time on and off the paid clock, just to talk with them. The staff had been encouraged by Sam and Craig who were jealous and angry. They watched me like vultures unable to find anything to report me on. They were supposed to report all the dirt they dug up on me to Sam, but they not only had nothing bad to say, they were enraged at seeing the progress I was making, all the while seeing all the good I was doing. They believed me to be too care free. Patients admitting they needed help and drew out only my deepest respect for them. Other staffers either didn't care or were burned out. I was consistently genuine, even if it cost me my internship. I demonstrated humanity in the most basic form and it pissed people off. You must be grounded on planet Earth in some way, because there isn't a procedure to follow for every situation you'll encounter in life. When a state of affairs isn't black and white, you should follow your instincts.

On another eventual day, I saw a young lady who was diagnosed with Borderline Personality Disorder by the psychiatrist. People with this disorder can be very intensive in relationships and contrary.

After the second session, she moved her chair right up to me, wrapped her legs around me very quickly and said, "You're so sexy."

I immediately went into cardiac arrest! She had a vice grip like an anaconda. After extracting myself from her grip, I informed her that I needed to transfer her to a female therapist. She went from, "You're so sexy" to

"I hate you and hope you die!"

My thoughts were that if I remained in the internship, she may get her wish. Since I was too inexperienced to handle the situation and my supervision was next to nil, I thought of handing her off to Sam … or better yet, to Craig. But again, I felt discretion was the better part of valor.

Meanwhile, another doctoral intern started at the hospital from my school, giving me a feeling of camaraderie. This intern did exactly what was asked of her, even if it had a distressing effect on the patient. She said she needed to do whatever she needed to do to get through the program and graduate. When I challenged her on this, she emphatically told me not to bring any problems to her either. She said she heard of my reputation as a black sheep and she knew most of the staff were burned out and overworked.

"Besides," she explained to me, "The psychiatric units in hospitals were much worse in the 1960's and 1970's and we've progressed."

"So this was progress?" I asked her.

She ignored me and said, "Good luck."

As she said this, I turned and looked behind me. Two men and three women were holding an angry, red faced lawyer on the floor while sedating him and preparing to place him in a strait jacket. "Progress I muttered?" One woman was holding the patient's neck down with her foot, while another male had his knees on his back. I guess this was standard procedure.

He was then transferred to a padded room while yelling, "I'll sue! I'll sue!" I was stunned after seeing this.

The following week, I went to see him, but he had been discharged! I went into the padded room to look where he had been. I closed my eyes to feel what it would have been like to be there in a strait jacket. As I opened my eyes, I saw a new nurse close the door and lock me in.

I ran to the meshed window and said, "Hey! I'm an intern. Let me out!"

"Sure you are," the nurse replied sarcastically and left the area immediately.

"Great," I thought.

This can't get much better unless they decided to now give me ECT treatments (Electroconvulsive Shock Treatment). I turned pale thinking about that.

Then I heard a voice call out saying, "Hey, you are my doctor-right?"

I looked behind me in surprise to see one of my patients behind me sitting on the floor.

I said cautiously, "Yep just here to check on you."

He replied "Thanks Doc. I always knew you cared."

I did later help to get him out of the facility and back home.

After a few minutes, Shawn looked in and said, "Whatchya doin' in there pal?"

I replied, "A nurse locked me in."

He turned around and laughed, "I told you not to hit on the nurses."

"Very funny, Shawn," I exclaimed.

He replied back, "They had you down for ECT today."

I wasn't laughing, because it might have been true. Later that day, I gave a beautiful polished stone to the lady with the cancer. I told her this usually brought me luck. Up until the time I worked here, however, so it was probably an omen by now. I gave it to her before she was discharged. I told her I wished her all the best luck in the world with it. We gave each other a tearful hug and she thanked me for "being there for her." I looked around to make sure Sam was not there.

I never knew what happened to her, but I caught hell from a doctoral level social worker who was supervising my friend, who registered disapproval because I gave a patient a gift again and gave a goodbye hug to her. This, I was told, created a boundary issue and of course, Sam made note of this ... again! I was again chastised. My school called and stated that if I did not work out in this current internship, they would relocate me. I held my breath.

Suddenly out of the labyrinth, Cal came to me the following week while I was nervously eating lunch with Tammy in the cafeteria. Cal had not taken a bath for three weeks, was unshaven and in pajama bottoms now. *I thought he must live in the neuropsychology lab.*

"Guess what?" Cal said to me excitedly. "I've got news you've been waiting to hear Doc," Cal said.

"You're killing me, what?" I asked him impatiently.

"What is it?" I repeated again.

"Your nemesis is gone ... really gone," he replied.

"You're freaking kidding me," I exclaimed to him in astonishment.

"She's gone. Sam is history. No more harassment!" Cal said excitedly.

Tammy was laughing and Kathy came by, patted me on the back and said, "Congratulations, Tom. You are free man!"

They all laughed as I breathed a sigh of relief. Tammy had completed her time and moved on! I gave her a good report to my supervisor and she received credit for her internship. She wished me well and told me she would keep in touch. I never heard from her again. Shawn felt psychologists didn't seem to have the respect M.D.'s had and decided to pursue medical school after receiving his Ph.D. in psychology. I bought him a strait jacket for his birthday present and threatened to lock him in the padded room with Sam. He was not amused.

The charge nurse informed me that my supervisor, Casper the Ghost, wanted to see me.

After putting down his golf clubs, he said to me, "We've got problems."

"We've?" I asked him as anxiety welled up in me. "What does we've mean?"

"Sam wrote an intense complaint letter, a poison pen letter," he told me, concerning his level of supervision and every mistake she perceived I made in my internship. I'm thinking, *what supervision?*

She said in her letter that she even had asked the nursing staff and security staff to keep an eye on me, and to take notes. I think I turned blue from hypoxia at this news. I was absolutely stunned! While I thought I was home-free, he informed me that she took it upon herself to be judge, jury, and executioner, writing letters to my school, my supervisor and the administration at the hospital. When I asked my school for a copy of the letter to respond to, in my disbelief, the intern coordinator replied,

"Sorry, Tom, I can't do this. Get a copy from your administrator."

I was told by my Dean, "We just hope the hospital will allow you to finish after what was reported."

I felt as if a train had just hit me head on with Sam as the engineer grinning from ear to ear. The train would have been more merciful. Adapting an old saying I'd heard fit perfectly; "It takes six men to carry an intern named Tom to his grave and one woman named Sam to put him there." Not only did she solicit comments from Craig, a reliable source indeed, but from nurses as well. One nurse she enlisted was the charge nurse who had mixed feelings about my techniques, such as standing on my head to get a patient to comply with medication. I went up to a psychiatrist relaxing with his feet up on the desk, while being given coffee by a nurse and calmly asked him for cyanide. I thought it reasonable; however, when he refused my request, he told me to get a life.

I said, "I'll settle for a cup of coffee."

The nurse told me where the pot was and where to go. When I got there, it was empty. Since I didn't get my cyanide or coffee, I decided to write a rebuttal letter to my school and the hospital administration. My supervisor wrote a letter as well and we were eventually exonerated. A small contingent of nurses threw me a party.

One nurse said to me, "You are what mental health is all about. You are our unsung hero."

Hearing those words, they're recognition of what I had gone through, brought a tear to my eye. Up until that moment, I felt betrayed, victimized and rejected, just like the patients. Kathy, Shawn, Cal and some of the doctors and nurses applauded. They gave me gifts as they wished me well. Some hugged me as Kathy spoke to me.

She said as she put her arm around me, "To always be me" and to "Walk my own path in life."

I was told that Kathy one day walked into the ladies room and saw Sam crying uncontrollably. When she asked what was wrong, Sam wiped her tears and said, "Nothing," as she walked out of the ladies room. My heart softened and I realized that people who projected anger are hurting people who need love the most. Unfortunately, hurt people hurt people.

When I graduated with my doctorate degree in clinical psychology, a small contingent of my classmates stood up and applauded shouting, "Go Tom!" as if I was running for a touchdown. I teared up but tried to hold it back. But it had a mind of its own and tears ran down my cheeks. Until my tears started to flow uncontrollably, I hadn't realized until that moment how long they'd been built up. I was destressing. My classmates had heard of my struggles in my internship and wished me well. They quietly relayed their disappointment in the school for not being supportive, but realized that the goal was to ultimately graduate. One of our esteemed professors told us at our graduation that if he were to become a psychologist again, he would not do it. He exclaimed he would be damned if he would allow managed care to tell him how much to make, what diagnostics to make, what testing he could do, etc. and etc.!

Mark, one of our fellow graduates, yelled out, "Thanks for telling us now that we're only $90,000 in debt!"

I quickly reconsidered ACME trucking school again. I was officially a "Doctor" now unemployed and $90,000 in debt. I still needed to do a post-doctoral residency and, of course, pass the infamous psychology licensing exam called the "E Triple P," or The Examination for Professional Practice in Psychology, the bane of many psychology students. It was about this time when I talked with my father and told him some of my stories, omitting names, times and dates of course. He encouraged me to write a manuscript or a book. This book would help to give others a glimpse of the mental health world and also hopefully shine a light on a need for more mental health services. He could not believe the things that happened and always asked if I had more new stories.

He followed up with, "So did you help anyone today?"

Sometimes, I did. He was pleased with this and told me to always to be empathic to those who needed the help the most, never judgmental. My father appreciated and respected educated people primarily because he felt that with an education one could help society more. He did not have a college education and for him to have two "doctor" sons made him, as he would say, "as proud as a peacock". He used to take the neighborhood kids to ballgames and pay for everything, while telling them to go to school and learn as much as they can. I miss my father very much to this day.

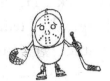

YODA

CHAPTER FOUR

A new graduate and officially a Doctor of Psychology, I applied to several post-doctorate placements. Three out of twelve of those I applied accepted me for placement. One of the three placements I was offered was at a psychiatric hospital. Having just finished an internship at a psychiatric hospital, you can imagine at this point how I felt about taking that placement, especially when I had other options. That offer was a big no! Another offer came from a forensic hospital for the "criminally pathological". Patients at this facility were considered NGRI (Not Guilty by Reason of Insanity). I thought I would gain great experience. Residents were mostly murderers, rapists and those that thrived on physically or emotionally harming others. People one would naturally think of inviting to a party. The wing I would be working in was very dismal, dark and quiet, kind of like my internship. The facility was far from my home, so I ultimately decided against it. I didn't feel it would be a good fit for me, especially since I enjoyed living and breathing.

I accepted a position at a religiously affiliated facility for conduct-disturbed children. Although I noticed some "normal dysfunction" at the facility, I was assigned a supervisor of incredible magnitude. He worked with Dr. Carl Whitaker, studied at the University of Chicago who studied more theories than I realized existed. My new mentor was a bit flamboyant, especially in his manner of dress. Wearing a trench coat, wide brimmed Australian Bush hat and multi-colored shirts, he was called "Yoda" by the other post-doctoral students. Ben was slightly overweight, easy going and down to earth. He had a huge smile to match. He had soft grey hair, piercing emerald eyes, and a roundish face which lit up when he talked about psychology. Ben was indeed the "Jedi Master." I called him "Obi Wan Kenobi" as I presented him with a Yoda doll he could put on his desk. He was humble, but brilliant. I was more of a Luke Skywalker trying to soak it all in. Sometimes you could feel Ben's presence even when he was not in the facility. When bombarded by the usual insanity of the mental health profession, I would sit quietly in Ben's office to feel his essence to calm me down. I bonded with Ben and him with me. I decided to stay two more years after my residency ended, to learn from him all I could. As dark as my previous experience was, this one had magic in the air.

Ben was a storyteller encouraging me to tell these fantastic stories to the children I conducted testing, intakes or psychotherapy with. He used brilliant metaphors. He'd caution me about certain people; encouraged be to bring a toy lizard, which changed colors, as an illustration of what he was saying.

"The lizard was a chameleon and would not always be what it seemed. It changed colors as do people," he said.

He illustrated this with staff members, patients-anyone who'd benefit. Ben said I reminded him of the man who walks down the street and falls into a pothole. The next day he walks down the street, anticipates the first pothole and goes on to fall into another pothole.

"When you have fallen into enough potholes," he said, "you will figure it out and just walk down a different street."

He said this is illustrative of how I learn: through experience. Ben taught me magic tricks to use with children to hold their attention, and to use subtle ways to manipulate positive change through redirection. He reaffirmed that giving and receiving gifts, small gifts, was not a crossing of boundaries as my previous internship supervisors suggested. Instead, that was a meaning of a valued relationship, providing you don't accept a Lexus in return. I found Ben enthralling and numinous.

One day, Ben and I were walking to a group home which was managed by a specific denomination, whose clergy were driving new Cadillac Escalades.

"Somehow, I don't think we would be seeing Mother Theresa driving an Escalade around Calcutta while she visits the poor, do you?" Ben asked me.

He talked about being true to oneself rather than being false to one's theology. The state closed this facility because of suicides and fiscal spending that was not accounted for. Ben was spiritually wise, studying theology himself. We discussed how many wars were fought in the name of religion. I didn't allow myself to be caught up in group hysteria or groupthink situations, such as the Salem Witch Trials. He supported my learning to think critically, independently, and above all: not to lose sight of whom I was. He would say life is movement and don't ever look back.

He and I took walks together around a beautiful lake on campus. Occasionally, he would bring lawn chairs so we could sit and watch baby ducks with their mothers. Beautiful blue Herrings would fly gracefully above the water while I would absorb his wisdom. It is easy to bond with him. We spent so much time together, I wondered if I was his favorite student. He taught me about "me", recognizing my heart was in the right place. I also learned how to relax. If you allow yourself to be caught up in the drama of people, you'll live in perpetual suffering.

"Learn to accept that it is inevitable, learn to not be caught up in it, and learn to handle it with grace," Ben would say.

I never saw him angry. He was a bright light in a dim forest. He discussed martial arts, Buddhist philosophy, and history with ease. He was always doing charitable things for others.

When I was walking toward a group home with Ben one day, I felt something slam my shoulder with a huge thud. I looked back and saw excrement on my shoulder. I thought a Pterodactyl defecated on me.

"Looks as if you have been inadvertently pooped on," Ben said.

We looked up and saw a young child throwing excrement down from a bucket to whoever came within target range.

Ben told me, "Apparently, they pooped on this child and he was literally pooping on them."

We laughed together and the child yelled, "Sorry Dr. Tom. I didn't mean to hit you. I'll have to adjust my aim."

The goon squad at the facility soon removed him and gave him a much-needed bath.

Another incident involving a psychiatrist at the facility and a child got into a verbal altercation.

Ben and I watched as Ben said "Learn from this as to what not to do!"

Ben said. The child called the psychiatrist every name he could think of and the psychiatrist chased him around a table calling him names back. Finally, the goon squad came, grabbed the child and took him away before the psychiatrist could hit him with an injection of Thora zine.

Ben laughed and stated, "Well, I thought that went well. Didn't you?"

I was so speechless with my mouth hanging open, I could've caught flies.

I had always driven older AMC Gremlins, but I was a "Doctor" now and was thrilled I could buy my first new car, a small brown Nissan Altima. I worshipped that car. It was brand new. *I thought I had arrived now that I have the means to buy myself a new car.*

I bought my first new car, during my post-doctorate internship. I was walking to my new car when I stood in horror as I noticed deep scratch marks on the hood and side of the vehicle on the door.

"You suck! I hate you! Die, you warlock!" and more expletives.

Next to my car was a new, black Mercedes Benz glistening in the sun, immaculate and untouched. *What could I have possibly done to bring this holocaust onto myself? Did I not conduct a magic trick with a child properly enough, or maybe I offended a psychopathic staff member? But how was that Mercedes not touched?* I didn't get it, but found out later it was the child who had the altercation with the psychiatrist. Again, he missed the correct target thinking that the Mercedes was mine and the Altima was his. When I confronted the child, who was now in isolation, heavily sedated, I told him M.D.'s drive Mercedes; new Ph.D.'s drive Pintos, Gremlins and Altima's just in case he ever wanted to re-attack a target. The facility was nice enough to pick up the cost of repainting my car and I decided to park my car in Australia, far from the facility, from then on.

There was a rather nice walkway around the campus, and a beautiful lake that I liked to occasionally walk or jog around. While jogging, I stopped to look in a rabbit hole with a mother tending her babies. *Well,* I thought, *there appears to be no mental health issues here.* As I proceeded to continue my jog before starting work, I noticed a bush gyrating violently. *What the...?* I thought. This bush was possessed and I immediately wanted to run to find a priest to conduct an exorcism on it. I feared for my life, and then I heard some moans. Approaching with caution, I noticed one of my kids with his girlfriend tripping the light fantastic.

He looked around, was startled and said, "Oh no, it's Dr. Tom. Are you going to turn us in? I'm screwed if you do."

"You've already been screwed. Do you have a condom?" I asked him.

He told me, "I always use protection, see?" as he pulled out two condoms from his pocket.

His girlfriend giggled and said, "Oh Johnny, come on."

I couldn't stop them. They would find a way to do it somewhere else and if I turned them in, it might be worse.

Walking out I heard the words, "He is cool. Is he your shrink?"

We did process this later during his ongoing therapy sessions that he had with me on a weekly basis.

I told Ben of the encounter with Johnny and his girlfriend. Ben told me that during my next session with Johnny to repeat to him, "A tisket, a tasket, a condom or a casket." Ben felt I did the right thing and advocated for protection rather than always prevention because,

"These kids will find a way, like nature."

We could do our best, but can't be with them 24 hours a day. Ben believed that gaining a good relationship with them was the key.

He said, "Power and control and disrespect equal war while respect, mutuality and cooperation equal peace. It's like the story of the two wolves, one angry, and one peaceful, who are in contest with each other."

When I asked who won the contest, he said, "The one you tend to feed the most, of course."

"Of course," I replied.

"Duh!"

Ben further told me of an old Chinese saying.

"Remember the greatest warrior is the one who can win without a battle. Always strive to teach and offer suggestions. Do not necessarily tell people things," he suggested.

I respected Ben's kindness, gentle manner and ultimate brilliance. My time spent with Ben taught me more about human behavior and how to reach out to people than the four years of being in the doctoral program. As Ben did with me, I would take kids out of the office and walk with them, play basketball, chess, work therapy through music, crafts and art or gardening. I did what I could do to reach them using Ben's techniques.

I observed younger staff members, basically kids themselves in their early 20s, wrap up the young residents in carpets and allow other children to play "kick the carpet," while other staff passed gas in the faces of the kids as a joke. Staff members would punish the residents for disobeying rules by taking away privileges such as their radios, television and video games. Suggestions were disregarded and I was generally chastised by many staff members for my techniques, saying that I was too easy on them. Ben told me to engage those staff members and offer proposals while allowing their input to give them a sense of empowerment.

"Cooperate with the staff, ask them for input and ask them to develop the plan and agree to tweak it," Ben said.

Things did progress in a mutually cooperative manner as Ben had suggested and positive changes were implemented. I was told to praise their efforts and I did. It took time but good things are worth the wait.

I was watching baby bunnies by the lake. I saw the babies, but not the mother as I peeked into the rabbit hole. I looked back and saw a horrifying site …rabbit attack! I jumped in the lake as the mother was running at me like a German U-boat from World War Two.

Motherly instinct? I guess she felt I was hurting her children. As I proceeded to climb out of the lake, I was dive-bombed by two mallard ducks. In my escape from Mrs. Rabbit, I apparently jumped into a near nest where ducklings were. Nature was going mad on me. Where was Marlon Perkins when I needed him? I was attacked on all sides. I ran to my office and locked myself in. I could have sworn I saw a duck fly by my window thumbing its nose at me as I looked out my office window. Recuperating in my office from my run-in with nature, I suddenly heard groaning and moaning. Were these moans and groans coming from a nearby bush again? Was this Johnny and his girlfriend? I had to check on the noises. They were not Johnny and his girlfriend and they were not from a bush outside. The sounds were coming from a married case worker/group manager who occupied the office next door to mine. I peaked in and Kinsey would have been proud. I gently closed the door and returned to my office quietly.

"Who am I to interfere with the natural order of things around here?" I exclaimed.

The case worker later told me she felt I was in my office a bit earlier than she expected and for my "silence" I could "do her" anytime I wanted. I passed on the opportunity, but assured her she need not worry about me. I had more important issues on my mind. She trusted me because I never betrayed her and she generally went to bat for me at this facility. With my share of conflicts in the way I felt staff treated the children, I was appreciative of her help.

I conjured up the courage to discuss a concern with the clergy, who had a bottle of whiskey on his desk. Maybe he was self-medicating. I did not see him and left without him seeing me.

I told Ben what had happened. Of course, he had plenty to say.

"Discretion was the better part of valor. You are learning about organizations. Don't exhibit foolhardy courage, but instead, thoughtful planning."

He emphasized this point with the story of two frogs that were standing on the edge of a bucket of milk. One jumped in thinking swimming in milk would be fun and accidentally knocked the other one in as well. The one who jumped forgot he couldn't swim, became frustrated and exhausted, didn't think straight and gave up and drowned. The other frog remained calm, thought his way through the situation, swam around, and around, and around until he churned the milk into butter and climbed out. Enough said; lesson learned I thought.

The following day I was walking around the campus and one of my kids ran up to me and stated he was leaving the campus and a car would be here to pick him up. I said I did not hear that he was officially discharged.

He told me, "It's not official Doctor T."

Before I could say anything more a car pulled up next to us with several adolescences in it. One jumped out and pulled a "Zip Gun" on me. It looked like a toy and I found out later it was a homemade gun which fired a real bullet, hence the term Zip Gun. My kid told the other youth to put his gun away. He said I was his doctor and that "I was cool." The kid with the gun called me "a smart Mother F etc.....," He so wanted to shoot me and his face betrayed a determined focus to do this. He looked me squarely in the eye and I could see the anger in his. He reluctantly put away the gun, deciding not to shoot me, and they drove away. At first I stood in shock trying to take it all in. Then, I informed the administration. Then realized I had to change my underwear, and felt that if my kid was not there I would not be here to write this.

I was shocked when I found out that this kid I was counseling who left in the car from the facility went back to his gang. I later heard he shot and killed his girlfriend who allegedly had affection for a rival gang member. The case manager wanted to go down to see him as did the others. Becoming somewhat of a three-ring circus, I decided to stay away. Feeling I had failed as a therapist, I was broken-hearted close to breaking down. I remembered what a professor at school once said to us, "When you lose a patient in any way, shape or form, you must have done something wrong and have to reevaluate."

I ran this by Ben who did not agree.

"There are influences you cannot always foresee or control," he stated. "Pick up your pieces, learn and move forward. Don't ever look back and have regrets. You cannot change the past, learn from it, only the present and its impact on the future can be dealt with."

Ben always had a way of comforting me and putting situations into perspective. He certainly brought a sense of logic and common sense to a somewhat chaotic world at the facility, bringing me balance. I felt that life at this facility was a bit surreal. Ben stated, however, that mental health, medicine, education, and the legal profession all have their share of drama and chaos. This facility was all too real in how it mirrors life. It was really about people and how they act and react per needs. He taught me that, what I was doing was re-parenting, but went into depth I couldn't truly understand at the time. He offered me a book to read which put things into perspective, <u>The Drama of the Gifted Child</u>," by Dr. Alice Miller. Dr. Miller's book clarified things for me. I read her subsequent books with zeal. People hurt others because sometimes they have been hurt and act out of unmet needs. Victims of abuse sometimes abuse others because of perceived weakness or projections of feelings they perceive in others which may remind them of a part of themselves. They rebel and resent those weaknesses which put them in the situation they couldn't control or escape. Hurt people do indeed hurt people. To paraphrase the magnificent ophthalmologist turned psychologist, Dr. Alfred Alder, theories today may essentially change tomorrow. These were interesting theories and appeared to make sense, at least for today. Human behavior is purposeful.

One day, a clerical worker rushed up to me and said excitedly, "Dr. Tom, you'll be getting a new kid to see, but he's not your typical 'gang-banger', conduct disorder kid."

"What do you mean?" I asked her with a reticense.

She left as quickly as she came in. I was feeling wired, so I decided to go over to Dr. Warren's secretary. She was an easy target for my jokes. Dr. Warren was the psychologist in charge of the mental health part of the facility and my boss. Jane was a pretty girl, about 25 years old and just about every male at the center flirted with her. She had lovely soft features and a flawless complexion. She had red hair which beguiled an easy attitude. I always loved trying out new material on Jane and getting her to burst into uncontrollable laughter.

Even Dr. Warner told me, "Leave Jane alone. Three minutes with you and she becomes a useless blob of Jell-O the rest of the day."

Jane suddenly looked at me and Dr. Warren and laughed loudly. After my fun with Jane, I went back to my office stepping over a child along the way that was being held down by four female staff while throwing a tantrum. I came back with his favorite treat and exercised Grandma's rule, also called, The Premack Principle.

"You can have your treat if you behave as you're expected" I told him, and we talked about how to behave.

He was released from bondage as per my instruction, calmed down, complied with what he was told and given his treat with future expectations paired with future treats. I was thanked by staff and gave them treats as well. I figured it couldn't hurt.

On my days off, I spent time down the street at the local airport dreaming of taking up flying. I watched with envy aircraft gracefully landing, buffeting the wind like a sailboat cranking her main sails into the wind and I watched the effect. This quickly became my favorite way to relax. I wondered what it would be like to fly on the wind and leave the earthly shackles and be free for a time. I decided to bring some model boats, cars and planes for the kids to build the following week, hoping to inspire them and keep them focused on more constructive tasks. The group homes would reimburse me for this, but it wasn't about the money. I eventually formed a model club with some of the kids too. For me, this was as heavenly as flying.

The call I had been dreading finally came. That special kid I had been told about had arrived and was waiting for me in my office with his case worker. I did not have any prior information other than he suffered a facial injury. Soon I would also get another who had been set on fire by his step-father, suffering 75% burns on his face and body. He wore a body suit made of some spandex material or such. Did I have a sign on me saying "I'll take the worst you got"? I felt incredibly ill-equipped. But I had my mentor, Ben, to help me out! And help me he did! Ben guided me with both boys and even conducted a magic magical session with one of them. This was a way to reach them and provide distraction from their issues. In this way he provided productive avenues for their anger.

I strolled nonchalantly to the front office to meet my new kid. As I entered the room I froze. I tried to hide my fear and anguish. Four feet in front of me sat a kid with only half a face. His right side was literally missing and he wore a partial phantom of the opera mask to hide his disfigurement. He was called the phantom by the kids, teased unmercifully. I tried to speak, my mouth was open, but no voice came out.

I finally stuttered, "Wh...wh...what happened?" Intense fear suddenly overwhelmed me.

I felt like Dr. Fredrick Treves the first time he set his eyes on the elephant man, Joseph Merrick. My heart broke for this kid. I cursed the bullying of other children, teasing and brutalizing others who were hurt, weak or different. My logic hit my emotional wall, and the wall won.

This child, who was now 15 years old, told me a few years back, he and his girlfriend "got high". They were playing with a loaded shot gun. While under a drug induced state, he asked her to shoot him and she complied, taking off half his face in the process. He was lucky he wasn't killed. Various surgeries were performed, but only with moderate success, thus the mask. I shook his hand and agreed to start counseling with him the following day after he settled in. In the meantime, I studied all his medical, physiological and psychological case files available to me.

I discussed the case with Ben who told me to "Act in opposite."

I said in a confused manner, "What?"

I thought Ben was hitting the communion wine while the clergy were off in their Escalades.

"Don't pay attention to the insult, because you'll miss the child," he reported.

"Pay attention to the child and you will win."

Halloween was coming and Ben told me to walk around campus with him.

I told Ben, "He said he feels like a freak and feels miserable."

Ben told me that misery loves company and you might want to think of being a freak yourself and join him. Ben was now speaking in tongues.

"I don't' get it," I replied.

Ben said, "You don't' exactly fit in yourself here, because you do things that are funny, different, and you tend to do and try creative things, right?"

"Right I think, so …?" I asked him.

He replied "So be a freak; get a mask and walk around campus with him too."

So I bought a hockey mask, like goalies wear. We would be freaks together. Normalize his pain.

In the meantime, a young man who was threatening suicide was waiting in my office. When I got there, he opened the window in my office, got angry and threatened to jump.

"I will," he shouted. "I will Dr. Tom, don't push me."

"I won't push you," I replied, "You're capable of jumping yourself."

"Go screw yourself," he stated, and started to go out my window to jump.

"You don't care do you?" he stated as he stared at me in disbelief.

"I can't stop you if that's what you really want," I stated again.

Just then, the door opened and a female aid came in.

"Joey," she yelled, "Don't jump!"

As she came through the door, Joey threw himself out the window. She screamed and ran outside. I calmly walked over to the window, looked down and saw Joey looking up at me. The window was only 5 or 6 feet off the ground.

I asked him, "Are you done playing now Joey? You scared the pants off Jill, the aid."

He replied, "Okay Dr. Tom, I'll come back in now."

"Good boy, Joey," I replied. "Now let's get back to work,"

I came back to my office the next day only to find the burned boy waiting for me. As I opened my office door, he sat there quietly, patiently looking at me in his black spandex suit complete with hood.

"Why hello," I said nervously.

Nothing came from this hooded figure whose eyes appeared dark from behind his sunglasses.

"I'm Dr. Tom. It's nice to meet with you," I told him.

His case worker came down and said, "I see you met Trevor, Dr. Tom."

I replied, "Yes, we were just getting acquainted," *at least I was I thought.*

She stated that she had to take him to see the psychiatrist for a medical evaluation and she would bring him back later.

I said, "Okay Trevor, see you later guy."

No smile. Nothing! Just a blank stare!

I bought a bag of peanuts to take a break and relax for a bit and went outside to play with the squirrels. I think the squirrels understood me. Periodically, I would fish with the kids by the lake and we would catch and release blue gills. We would see the squirrels come out and we would throw peanuts to the squirrels. After a while, I (using food as reinforcement) conditioned the squirrels to the fishing area. I even had one squirrel grab a peanut out of my hand. This took patience, trust and a very calm demeanor. While I was doing this, I heard someone behind me cough. The squirrel ran away as I looked back. Trevor was watching me with the squirrels. I gently told him to come forward and I gave him a peanut. I told him to crouch down and hold his hand out. After a bit of time, my friend the squirrel ran up and took the peanut. The squirrel, my co-therapist, won Trevor over and he agreed to see me in therapy. Later during supervision, I found out that Ben had been quietly watching me from a distance.

"Brilliant, my boy," Ben exclaimed! "I didn't know you had a way with squirrels," he said. "Now that you have him hooked, Trevor, not the squirrels, work to build your relationship with Trevor," Ben said.

The next day, I was shooting baskets with a female staff member at the gym. A man who was probably in his 60's walked slowly in the gym giving baseballs to a few of the children who were there. *I've never seen this guy before,* I thought to myself. *Who is he and why is he giving kids baseballs?* The kids ran out of the building to show off the balls they received to others. This man turned to me, smiled and waved. I waved back and smiled. He held out a ball for me.

I politely said, "No thanks." *What would I do with a baseball?* This is probably a volunteer from a nursing home giving kids baseballs.

He smiled as he said "Have a nice afternoon young man," turned and quietly walked out of the gym.

A few minutes later, another doctoral resident, Randy, came up and said, "Hey Tom, have you seen the professional baseball player yet from the Cubs?"

I said, in astonishment, "You mean that kindly older gentleman I just talked to, he is the baseball player from the Chicago Cubs from the 1960's and 1970's that guy?"

Randy said "Yep. Have you seen him? He's giving out autographed baseballs."

I just ran outside the gym yelling, "I'm insane, I'm insane, hey older baseball player come back!"

He drove off in a beautiful car, waving as he went. I never got an autographed baseball. Randy's suggestion about electroconvulsive therapy seemed a bit more appealing.

Halloween was coming. It was hockey mask time. People stared but no one said much of anything. This was my chance to help him relate to people again, to fight that seclusion his physical injury kept him in. I'd wear any costume to help normalize this boy's pain. One day of relief for him was the least I could do.

One treacherous evening, we almost lost him. He escaped (eloped) with a friend and two girls. They managed to get alcohol and found themselves on a railroad track where, the boy's male friend explained the two girls they fled with were encouraging him to sit on the tracks and kill himself. They wanted to see what the train would do to him. The male friend tore him off the tracks minutes before the train came whizzing by. The girls just laughed. Thank God someone was capable of being a human being and saved him just in time. I was stunned to hear that girls wanted to see a human being die. This was scary. *I'm thinking, their future husbands are doomed.*

He and I continued in our therapy sessions until the day he left. We said goodbye as he held me, tears intermingled. I watched him go, and I'd wondered how much I helped him. It was a miracle he was still alive, after all those kids had put him through. That was miracle enough for me.

Saturdays were my therapy days, watching airplanes at the local airport. I ached to learn to fly. I told Ben about my yearning to fly. He was cautiously optimistic.

He said, "Flying is heavenly, but I would not want you to be an angel before your time … if you get my meaning."

I understood his implied message.

Monday came and I was back at my post-doctoral residency, sitting quietly with Trevor. He agreed to come to therapy. He didn't agree to talk. Sitting in the silence,

I knew he was testing me, controlling the situation. An entire session of 45 minutes was filled with silence. I screamed my head off as soon as I knew he was gone.

Our aid Kathy came down and said, "Are you okay Tom?"

I said "Fine, I'm considering a singing career."

She replied, "Oh really. Can I offer a suggestion? Please Doc, do us all a favor and stay with psychology," she replied and left laughing out loud down the hall. Staying quiet for me was like pulling my teeth without Novocain. Just because it's doable doesn't mean it should be done.

The next day I was skipping rocks on the lake while Ben sat in his lawn chair. He was giving me feedback on my methods of interaction with the kids. He would never chastise me with condemnation if he disagreed with me. He was so cool.

"I have begged to differ, with your permission." He would say to me.

You never felt criticized or undermined. He was kind and warm, telling me to mirror exactly what Trevor did in therapy. Patience and respect is what he and you both require. Of course, I understood what Ben was trying to teach me. As usual it took me time to catch up. The fun began however.

When Trevor looked out a window, so did I. When he whistled, so did I. When he rocked in his chair, so did I. Then he started to talk to me.

"You're just doing what I'm doing," he stated with frustration.

Speech at last, I thought.

"And what's wrong with that?" I said back with a snappy response.

"Nothing," Trevor replied, "But you should really be your own person," he stated.

There was intelligence behind those dark sunglasses after all. We started to dialogue more and more every day. One day, he excused himself to go to the bathroom. The door hadn't closed all the way, and I was curious to finally find out what he looked like. I saw him for the first time in his reflection in the mirror. I saw his scared-bubbled flesh, dark, red and burned. It was horrible. He quickly turned and looked back sensing a voyeur, and I ran back into my room, aghast at what I had witnessed. I heard a door shutting and the turn of a lock. He'd locked the bathroom door.

I told Ben what I saw. He told me to give this child the deepest of respect and love, and honor his secrecy, saying "When you do this, you honor him."

Trevor finally confided in me about his mom. She would not stand up to his abusive alcoholic stepfather. Trevor was trying to protect his mom from his stepfather beating her again, and his stepfather, in a rage, doused Trevor with gasoline and set him on fire. His mother watched, saying absolutely nothing. It was so vivid in my mind. Suddenly, in the middle of our session, Trevor screamed, jumping out of his chair and huddling on the floor of my office. I met him where he was. I held him right there on the floor, rocking him through tears. We mourned together the loss of his childhood, his innocence. He hoped his stepfather would fill the void he had from his absent biological father and was disappointed. Then, he hoped his mother would protect him, trusting her to do so. And she failed him too.

Instead of visiting the squirrels, I diagramed on paper what transpired and the psychodynamics of this case to show Ben. He complimented me on my work and was so impressed by the diagram; he used it to teach other graduate students how to visually conceptualize a case. He thought it was brilliant, said I had natural instincts.

Ben warned, "Don't let this get to your head though."

After everything that's happened, why does everyone love to hate me in the profession? Of course, I went to my Jedi.

"Why the heck do people in the mental health profession beat me up?"

He laughed and said, "Two things. One, it's not just the mental health field and don't feel so honored or special. I've been abused in the field as well, and I've been in it longer, more abuse over a longer span of time. Secondly, understand that people who generally come into the field are seekers."

"Seekers?" I inquired.

"They indirectly seek advice, guidance, support or nurturance from the profession. They are sometimes angry, hurt, fearful, and have suffered abuse themselves. With individuals like this, it is important to be supportive, but also set adequate boundaries and always strive to teach."

Again, I think…*where the heck does he pull this stuff from?* Somehow, this made the pain of dealing with staff a bit more palatable. Ben suggested I read the poem *"Anyway"* by Mother Theresa. It helped, as if it voiced the pain I didn't quite know how to verbalize myself. Everyone strives for some form of significance; some in useful ways, some in not so useful ways. Ben taught me that a knowledgeable man knows others, but a wise man knows himself. Strive to be wise.

I also read a short poem called "The Desiderata," by Max Ehrmann. I read this several times along with the Serenity Prayer. For me to help others, I first had to come to terms with who I was, embrace my own demons. Things are not always, what they seem. Perceptions are not always reality. This was an echo from someone though. Strive for insight. Be patient and wise. This I learned from Jedi Ben!

One day, I went into cardiac arrest. Ben mentioned retirement on one of our regular walks around the pond.

"Leave the profession?" I protested in vain.

He said he wouldn't live forever and the umbilical cord would have to be cut at some point. He was on a spiritual journey and the journey needed to continue, but in a different way. He talked about Southeast Asia, Tibet, Buddhism, etc. He was on a continual journey of self-discovery and saw me on a similar path.

"Be curious, and behold the wonder of life, I have a passion for living and living things for which we are all connected," he explained. Remember to breath too, he said as he laughed. So many people forget to breathe when stressed. I feel it is necessary he said. I replied, Yeah, or you die. Absolutely, he replied as we both took a deep breath together. He knew this relaxed me.

One day, Ben was not at the site. I panicked! He wouldn't have left already without telling me. My site director told me Ben had a bad heart attack and was in the hospital. Dr. Warren told me he was okay, that we had a group card to send him. I thought impulsively "group card like hell!" I'm taking the day off and going into the city to see him. I was pissed! How could my fellow post-doctoral students who Ben supervised not go down to see him; only send this card! I had to go sit in his office alone, close my eyes and calm down. It calmed me. I was embracing those little demons and getting in touch with my inner chipmunk. I breathed quietly, looked cautiously at the Yoda Doll. I ran outside and hailed a cab, heading downtown where all the lights were bright.

As I entered the hospital, I was smart enough to bring my little "Dr. Badge." When a nurse approached telling me visiting hours were over, I shot out my badge telling her I was a doctor … no lie … right? Thank goodness, she never asked me what type of doctor. I told her I would only talk briefly and just was checking on him. She let me pass, amazingly enough.

I started to strut down the hallway.

As I entered Ben's room, he was sitting up smiling and said, "Come in Tom."

"What are you doing smiling and sitting up?" I demanded.

"Should I be lying down with a frown?" He sarcastically laughed.

I said, "Very funny, how are you feeling?"

"I'm fine, just needed to change my diet. They roto-rooted me," Ben replied with humor.

He explained how they cleared some blockage in his arteries around his heart. This was his wake-up call, to make a lifestyle change he explained. I was angry that no one else came to visit, but Ben accepted this with a calm serenity.

With total tranquility, he spoke "Don't take it personally. I don't. They have busy lives. I understand. But you, Tom, stood apart. You have what I call active empathy for others. Your compassion is contagious, but please be patient and generous with others when you can."

I told him I was blessed to have him as a mentor, supervisor and above all, a friend. We talked for hours into the night. Ben soon got out of the hospital. The time to say goodbye had come, my tears came despite my effort to keep it in. He hugged me as he told me to go into the world with confidence, to always trust your instincts. He left the facility, sold his house and went to Cambodia.

My resignation soon followed. Ben's absence left my heart broken. Before he left, he gave me a crystal Buddha. I still have it to this day. He told me to continue the journey to discover myself.

"Be on a quest," he told me, "because all that we truly have is what we give to others" so says Lewis Carroll. A life well lived is one that has a positive impact on other lives, I felt.

I had to see his office one last time to say goodbye, even though he wouldn't be there. I had no idea how one man could have such an impact. I could never forget him. After resigning my position at the facility for conduct disturbed children, I applied for the position of clinical director of an outpatient rehabilitation/mental health center in another state. Perpetrated by the profession once again, no good deed goes unpunished. Soon after beginning, a counselor at the center threw a note on my desk.

Great, I'm being hit on now.

The note said, "Welcome, Dr. Tom, to the Narcissistic World of Stu."

Stu was my new boss. New to Management, Stu initially appeared to be one I could learn from in terms of management. I had just passed the grueling licensing exam to become a licensed clinical psychologist. Plop, plop, fizz, fizz, oh what a relief that is! My first advanced position. I was legendary in my own mind.

I soon realized I worked for a narcissist who micromanaged his staff to death. The staff was angry and complained about him behind his back. He sabotaged my meetings, yelled at staff in the hallways and, in front of others nonetheless, he even hit me in the back of my head several times with whatever objects were handy. He admitted he abused alcohol, but claimed he was in a 25-year recovery now.

He would say at meetings, "I want your opinion," but he never took those opinions to heart, always manipulating them as his own advice or suggestions. Deep down though, Stu was a hurting man, which contributed to him being a very angry man living in denial.

He expected me to change the staff, to make everyone "like" him. He would eat lunch during meetings in front of the staff, while he refused to allow staff to eat lunch during those meetings. During my clinical meetings, I would give a directive. Then he'd invariably changed it saying, "We are not doing that." Several female staff learned how to manipulate him. When I requested things from these staff members, they would go to Stu who directed me to take care of things myself. At a public event Stu asked me to attend with him in the guise of praising my work, he vented his frustration in public stating I was the worst psychologist he had seen. I found out later he used a similar tactic with other directors who had resigned.

A staff member pointed out, "Stu goes through clinical directors like water through a hose." I was next on his hit list I felt.

Stu was politically savvy however. He knew how to make appearances look good, especially in more public meetings except for the above lambasting I took.

Leaving approximately one minute before 5 o'clock to pick up my child from daycare, Stu stopped me at the door stating I was to give him the full 8 hours, not 7 hours and 59 minutes. I told him I was a psychologist and his clinical director, basically salaried management.

He snapped, "And I'm your boss."

Clearly our relationship was strained. He convinced others I was a poor clinical director, but I believe he had another agenda. A secretary, whom he refused to let visit her very ill son in the hospital, hated him with a passion. She threatened to sue him and he relented. Then the "dot war," began. What was the "dot war"? Stu had a big board near the front office with everyone's name was on it. When you were out, you moved your yellow dot to the "out" space. When you were in, you moved the dot to the "in" space. Stu demanded that people always move their dot signifying whether they were "in" or "out." He was the exception, of course. He never adhered to any of his own rules. My error was that I called him on it, and I was taken to task afterward. While continuing his bullying behavior, Stu also expected me to increase staff morale. A visiting social worker called him a "dry drunk." I bought him a gift on his birthday and put staff names on it. The gift cost $50.00, with only $5.00 given by staff members for the gift; I paid virtually the whole thing. To my surprise, he thanked the staff.

Frustration would eventually get the best of me with the "dot war."

One day, I saw he was out, but his yellow dot was on the "in" slot. I pulled the dot off with a note that if I was to help with morale, he, as director, was to model appropriate behavior himself. He proceeded, red-faced, to berate me. He called me stupid, informing me if I ever did a foolish thing like countermand his behavior again; he would fire me on the spot or the dot. Stu continued to be an abusive bully. Finally, driven to the very edge of my sanity, I complained to the board, who informed Stu. So much for confidentiality. When he had found out he'd been reported, he hit me with a newspaper yet again, hard enough to give me a migraine headache. I threw up, but unfortunately missed Stu. I told him never to hit me again; that this would be considered harassment! If I had not needed the job and salary, I would have left on the spot or on the dot.

Later, after he calmed down, Stu asked me to meet with one of his departments to find out why morale was low. He told me, "I'd better fix the problem or else."

I boldly asked, "Or else what?"

"Need I tell you?" he replied.

When I had my meeting with the marketing staff, they were quiet and refused to look at me. Did I smell bad? So I am thinking, *I am boldly going where no man has gone before.*

Several minutes into it, I had to ask, "So why are you guys all depressed?"

No response.

"Stu wants to know why your morale is low."

Again, silence.

Directly addressing the lead director, I said "Your staff doesn't feel you stand up for them Paul."

Paul finally spoke up and said, "They are right, I don't."

You could have heard a pin drop.

"What?" I exclaimed. "You admit it?"

"Of course. You see, if I stand against Stu, my job would be in jeopardy. He's probably mentally ill and we all know he is a dictator."

Sarcastically I said, "And your point?"

"If I stand up for my staff, I risk being fired. I'm not getting younger. Where is an over-the-hill MBA, CPA going to find another job?"

"I see your point," I said.

Everyone knew what the root problem was: Stu. They did not blame Paul.

"So, what can I do?" I said.

One of the ladies interjected, "Just service us as best you can."

"Or leave!" another blurted out.

Apparently, I was once again emasculated I took from this position new knowledge of organizational behavior, people in general, and narcissists.

I had no idea though how to report to Stu what had been said in the meeting. The staff begged me not to tell Stu the truth: that he was the problem. I told them I probably was crazy, but not certifiable. They laughed and thanked me for being the buffer.

The next day, Stu asked for a full report on the results of the meeting. To save everyone's jobs, I talked to him like a used car salesman on amphetamines. I thought I'd be an amazing used car salesman if this didn't go well.

"So, tell me what the problem is," Stu said in his usual stern manner.

"The problem is you, you garden gnome," I thought to myself, but the actual words came out in the form of excellent Bull Shit. "You see, Stu, they have been working overtime, they have been crunching numbers thinking of ways to cut costs and to increase the profit margin. Paul has been driving the staff hard because he wants to make you proud of his department. They truly love you in a way you could not possibly understand."

Talk about feeding one's narcissism.

I waited for a reply.

Silence.

Then I thought, *"I'm dead!"* I was already mentally clearing my desk.

Stu finally spoke, "I'll talk to Paul about easing up on his staff and reassure him everything will be alright."

Yes! It worked!

"You're too kind Stu, and you're the man."

A physician friend of mine who is an addictionologist stated that narcissists don't like themselves and feel inferior. They act in an opposite way as a compensatory behavior. This information was very interesting indeed.

Later that day, Paul took me out to lunch.

"Thanks Doctor T. We owe you."

"So now who's going to save me?" I said. As Paul smiled and patted me on the back.

I told the staff that while the patients are on break they smoke cannabis in the back of the facility. No one monitors them, I emphasized.

. One staff who put this together decided to monitor breaks. I also told them to try and modify their programming because something wasn't working. Unfortunately, another staff told Stu I was interfering with their program even though I was clinical director. This was part of my job. Stu told me to back off –so I did. Eventually, the monitoring fell off and patients went back to smoking cannabis in the back of the facility again.

One incident happened, while at another sight for another evaluation. I was sent to a local hospital to do an assessment on an alcoholic in the psychiatric unit for my center. While there, I met a psychiatrist who liked me, for whatever reason. They asked me if I might consider working for the hospital as a staff psychologist, though I'd take a pay cut. My words came out before I could even breathe.

"Yes, absolutely," I told him excitedly.

"Well, I'll talk to the director and I'll get back with you," he told me optimistically.

"God really does exist. This is my way out!"

No more irritable bowel syndrome. No more nightmares of Stu. Though I occasionally saw random acts of kindness at times, to say Stu was angry was an underestimation. I know there was a good person deep inside Stu. I wanted to try to reinforce those random acts of kindness whenever they would happen.

He did admit to the staff "I was a truly kind man".

Even though every other indication spoke otherwise, he gave me a pen and pencil set as a parting gift. I'm just happy it didn't explode after I took it home. I still have it too.

I took with me administrative knowledge from Stu on how to plan, organize and work a strategy. I understood his style was much too extreme and his staff turnover was ridiculous. The knowledge I gained for organizational management came at a price. In retrospect, I learned to control my emotions while under stress and turn a negative situation into a potentially positive one. I am empathetic to Stu and hope wherever he is, that he is more enlightened. Hopefully he's doing well. I truly do not wish anyone ill will. Then, The Dot War ended.

I transitioned to a hospital. My experience has been that medical facilities and hospitals tend to be rigid and hierarchical systems, highly punitive at times. The hospital vice president told me directly that physicians, those that are an M.D. or a D.O., are kings. Everyone else was a serf. This wasn't news to me. I was crowned with a medical badge and honorary white lab coat signifying that I now belonged to that special elite club. The white coat was status. People saw the Dr. Title, the white coat and holy roly poly, there was instant respect. When I took these adornments off, I was relegated to serfdom. The charge nurse thought I was an MD and absolutely gave up her chair for me and brought me coffee. Of course, I had my white esteemed coat on. Later that day, someone told her I was a psychologist … no chair, no coffee, and no room to even stand.

She stated, "Why are you even on medical staff? It's not like you're a real doctor."

Even some psychiatric nurses can be cruel at times. Hurt people, hurt people.

A visiting psychiatrist known to be very arrogant by others came on the psychiatric unit. I extended my hand to him as he turned in his chair and greeted me.

He asked, "So what specialty of psychiatry do you practice?"

I explained I was a psychologist. He immediately turned around on a dime and continued to chart his notes. It's not my cologne, not my smile … oh I got it. Yes! It was the small stain on my tie from the coffee I had not gotten this morning. Yep, that's it! I'll get a new tie and try again later! What is it that the joker said, "What does not kill you only makes you stranger?"

Later came, but this time he didn't even turn around. This is the same psychiatrist who gave his cat Risperdal and put him in a coma. I also met a social worker who was self-appointed as the unit manager. The social worker addressed me as Tom, told me to take off my lab coat and informed me I was not to round with the psychiatrists or medical students on the unit as I would violate patient confidentiality. But I was on the medical staff! My blood pressure must have elevated because I reflected a red glow on the white walls of the psych unit. I told her three things: (1) I was indeed a psychologist; (2) I could round with the psychiatrists because I was on medical staff and (3) She was not my boss. Then I breathed as Ben taught me.

She told me, "Tom, my say is final and you're done. Don't give me grief."

I went to the psychiatrist who helped me get into the medical center to plead my case. He was frightened for his own job and told me to calm down and let it go. I hoped gnats and fleas would infest the social worker's armpits. Hoping to learn more from the psychiatrist rounds, I left the unit dejected.

Later, however, this doctor did take me under his wing and let me round privately with him when the social worker was not around. How brave was that? I learned how diabetes, electrolyte imbalances and other medical conditions affect mental health status conditions.

On a rainy work day, I was headed to my office, and I found a kitten curled up by the door. I hid it under my lab coat and brought it into the facility. The office manager kicked me and the cat out yelling "no pets allowed!" No psychologists either obviously. I sat with the kitten under an enclave feeding it pieces of a candy bar in my breast pocket.

A lady came by and said, "Hello Doctor."

I looked back. Was she talking to me?

"Aren't you a doctor? It says that on your tag, you know. What a lovely kitten. Is it yours?"

She had a British accent. She told me she was visiting a friend who loved kittens. She said she had two kittens back in England herself.

I asked her, "Do you want a third?"

She smiled and said she couldn't take it back to the UK, but she would take it and see if she could find a home for it while she was here. I wondered if she could maybe find me a home too … in England! I thanked her for her kindness and told her she appeared mentally healthy.

She gave me a quizzical look and said, "I think you have been in the rain a bit too long Doctor. You best get inside."

She must have sensed my suicidal depressive state and said, "Life can't be all that bad you know. Think of all the positive things."

She patted me on the back saying "Goodbye, young doctor. Take care now."

As she disappeared into the English fog, I asked myself, "Who was that woman?"

Unexpectedly, Jaclyn who was the office manager, called me inside. She came from an alcoholic background and although outwardly jovial, I sensed her affect betrayed her inner mood. She was seconded by her secretary, Millie, a no nonsense type who had suffered domestic abuse from her partner. Together they were the queens of mean. As I often did, I thought of Socrates and longed for hemlock.

Jaclyn stated her rules to me: "Number 1: rules apply to you and the counseling staff, but not to the nurse practitioner, charge nurse or the two psychiatrists. They can write prescriptions; you can't. Number 2: You will not be called Doctor, even though you think you are one. Number 3: I'm the boss … I'm boss."

Basically, I couldn't piss without permission.

When I used the restroom, Millie yelled out in front of colleagues, "Quit peeing on the seat!"

On at least one occasion, I told her I had "not used the bathroom, but the psychiatrist was just there and suggested she confront him about it."

She remained noticeably quiet, not wanting to challenge a psychiatrist. *Remember, M.D. means M. Deity!* I thought. I reported this to Jaclyn how I was always the brunt of her jokes.

"You're too sensitive" She said. *Maybe I was?* I thought.

Indignantly after thought, I retorted "Maybe if you had encountered more people that are sensitive in your life, you might not be so angry."

She called me a "spoiled brat" as I laughed and shook my head. She slammed the door on me.

Then I *thought I'll kill them with kindness and so on Secretaries Day, I sent flowers to the staff, take them out for pizza.* However, the abuse continued. The hits kept on coming. No good deed goes unpunished. I felt like one of Pavlov's dogs conditioned by the staff; controlled, feeling helpless, disheartened and broken again. Was it jealousy? Was it that the staff interpreted my kindness as a weakness and it threatened them? I wasn't sure.

I had no raise in four years and no pay for all my public seminars I'd done. I was never paid for my on-call coverage, but the nurse practitioner was and the psychiatrists were. Despite experience I brought with me and a Ph.D., I was told I was making more than the nurse practitioner who recently just graduated and was on nursing staff. Later, I found that they paid him about fifteen thousand dollars more because he could write prescriptions. This was needed however and I realized this. He also received raises as did the psychiatrists. They would not allow me to sit down with the psychiatrist or the nurse practitioner to see the "spreadsheets." *I kept asking myself, why is this happening? Where's Rod Serling? Was I kissed by a vulture in my cradle? I'm cursed I thought.* Despite this I kept responding to calls by the nursing staff sometimes at three o' clock in the morning to come to the ER. I know the staff appreciated this. I was obsessed with my duty, or perceived duty.

I was extremely tired when I agreed to take on-call status for a psychiatrist. Although the psychiatrist was paid for this time, I was not. However, he did tell me over lunch the following week that he was appreciative of my covering for him. I was waiting in my office when the patient I was waiting for arrived. He was a police officer referred for anger management issues. When he arrived, he had a verbal altercation with Millie, a psych patient in her own right. He became angry and stormed out. Millie never alerted me that he had left. After several minutes waiting for him, I went to the front desk and asked where Joe was.

Millie stated, "He copped an attitude with me and stormed out."

"Where did he go?" I asked her out of frustration.

"I don't know, I don't care, he's not allowed back. I'll talk with Jacky about this," Millie replied back in an instant while looking away from me.

I ran outside and saw Joe at the back of his car. He opened the trunk and was grabbing his service revolver out of a case.

I said in a calm manner which hid my fear, "So how's it hanging Joe?"

Joe replied, "Outta my way Doc. I'm going to take care of that witch once and for all."

I said, "Joe, take a breath, calm down, talk with me."

Suddenly, I had a twisted thought of helping him load his gun, and then snapped out of it. Joe went on telling me how she insulted him, wouldn't listen and he felt attacked by Millie. I could relate. I encouraged him to put the gun back in the case, which he did. He broke down and cried and we took a long walk for an hour and a half. He gave me a hug and vowed not to hurt Millie, himself, or any others. I did inform the hospital security who later told me they would confiscate his weapon and told me to increase my therapy. There were more incidents and he eventually decided to leave the force. I never saw him again, but he was much improved overall. I truly was happy with this outcome. And yes, Millie was still breathing.

I realized that in this hospital culture, you could be chastised and marked if you asserted yourself vocally, even if in the patient's best interest. Management took notes as they watched from a distance. Paranoia thrived. You learned that you could voice your concerns and maintain ethical behavior, in which case you would lose your job, or you could stay under the radar. Most staff learned to play the game, bending ethics to survive. If you played the game, some staff members found themselves scapegoated and axed. The field was strewn with the bodies of the valiant, the peacemakers and the ones who became like the twisted systems themselves. It appeared that no one was safe from the dark side. Those working around management often became bobble heads bowing to the Queen-CEO, and her court. Not wanting to jeopardize their own jobs, there were those that were like sharks. They would turn on each other to save themselves. It truly was a dog-eat-dog culture. A senior vice president later verbalized this to me as he left because of what he called the "corrupt politics of the hospital."

As a stress reliever, I took up flying again. I bit the bullet and signed up for ground school at the local airport. After passing the tests, I signed up for the flight lessons.

I started lessons at the local airport on Saturdays and Sundays. I had always dreamed of flying. This was my therapy and I looked forward to my weekends. I took my first solo flight after my 10th lesson and I felt a sense of accomplishment and control. I met a pilot at the hospital and we became fast friends. He was also a therapist who reported having difficulty with the hospital as well. He eventually quit and litigated in a contract dispute. He won his case against the hospital and never looked back as his anger abated. We are still friends and fly together occasionally. Through my friendship with him, I became more self-aware. I woke up one day and looked straight ahead. Everything was clear.

I yelled loudly, "It's a miracle. I can see."

Okay, I forgot to take my contact lenses out the night before, but I did have more insight into myself. I wished my destination was as clear. I had a boxing match with my conscience: do the right thing vs. sit by and be quiet. I thought about what I had always been told; that evil prevails when good men do nothing. I thought about how evil prevails when good men do things anyway. I decided to survive. There was no support and I would throttle myself back a bit, be quieter. As the song goes, I'm alone again, naturally. I did not want to constantly be in the line of fire, yet I had to do the right thing and figure out how without being crucified.

Sitting near the hospital on the cement curb, I sat my empty coffee cup next to me as I closed my eyes to relax and center myself and to meditate. I controlled my breathing and relaxed for several minutes. When I opened my eyes, I looked up to see a woman standing over me saying, "Do I just put the quarter in the cup?"

"What are you talking about?" I asked her.

She said, "I know it's hard to be homeless" and put a quarter in my empty coffee cup and walked on. I must have appeared a bit disheveled and there were already six quarters in my cup. Business was good on the street. I wanted my old monkey back but he was probably in the Bahamas with that girl. So now who is the chimp or should I say Chump?

I decided not to wear my lab coat anymore, just my nametag. I was chucking off the sterility of the medical profession and its hard science; the science that distances itself from human feeling and emotion. I wanted to promote the softer science of psychology and close the gap between science and humanity. I wanted to connect to people on a more human level and to empathize with their pain. I wanted to understand them and attempt to give tools to cope; to give them hope. What is it they say…hope floats!

"Oh, the humanity," I blurted out, the Hindenburg explosion on my mind. I decided I would take the day off and went fishing with my brother. Since we caught no fish on the boat, we fished from the dock. It was only a few minutes before we decided to call it a day and go home. When I picked up my fishing pole, low and behold it contained a fish. As I lifted it onto the dock, the fish spit the hook out, righted itself and ambulated via pectoral fins after my brother and me. I had no idea fish could make noises like that. This was not a fish we had ever seen, but a demon spawn from Satan's lair. My brother had majored in biology before attending medical school but failed to identify this bizarre species. He agreed it was a hybrid between a human and a fish. Since it was apparently pissed off and was "walking" toward us, we both packed up our poles and drove away quickly from the lake vowing never to return. I can't speak for my brother, but this fishing trip was memorable and took my mind off of the hospital, if for a short time. That was one weird fish and we still laugh at how fast we drove away. My father told us we caught a Godzilla fish.

He laughed and said, "My big doctor sons afraid of a fish."

Wisdom comes from doing, from experience, whereas knowledge comes from reading. Ben once told me I had a passion for living and a reverence for life. Though Ben was on the other side of the world, he was still with me. No, I wasn't delusional. I knew he was on the other side of the planet. But, he remained with me in spirit. What he taught me kept coming back to me over and over; sort of like a mild form of obsessive compulsive disorder.

At work the next day, I was writing notes when the unit secretary introduced a new patient. A mysterious man came as a patient to my office. He only gave his first name, paid cash, no insurance and told me to take no notes. A plethora of potential diagnoses ran through my mind along with possible medications. He told me he used to be a spy and worked not only for our government, but other governments as well. I began formulating possibilities in my mind as conceivable diagnoses such as: paranoid disorder; paranoid schizophrenia; paranoid delusional disorder; schizotypal personality disorder, to name a few. This was the first time I was thinking in multiple diagnostic terms. When I arrived at work after his arrival, Millie informed me he was waiting in my office. I approached my office cautiously, slowly opened the door, looked around, even looked on the ceiling and did not see him.

I told Millie, "Oh, where is he? He's not in my office."

Millie said, "You're as bad as he is. We'll be putting you on meds Tom."

He was sitting on my couch when I went back to my office with Millie.

As Millie and I looked at each other, I said, "He wasn't there, honest."

"Just get to work and stop playing games doctor," she said sarcastically and chastised me.

Wow, I thought. *First time she called me doctor.* I looked to my patient.

"I was just in here and you weren't here," I said.

"I know how not to be seen Dr. Tom," he told me while smiling back at me.

"Don't play games with me pal," I told him, "I'm not sure where you were Mr. Spy, but please don't do that again or I'm not helping you … Capish?"

He smiled and stated "Everyone thinks I'm paranoid because people are following me."

I said, "Well, you're a spy, right? Of course, people are following you," thinking to myself schizophrenia and thinking about Risperidone or Haldol as possible medications. Then I thought, ok, we should conduct therapy under the infamous "Cone of Silence," like in the old Get Smart T.V. series.

During his third session, the paranoia was growing as he claimed his wife was going to leave him any day now. I had to write notes after he left every session. I tried to get him to agree to some tests but he became angry and lashed out.

"I could hurt you Doctor. I know martial arts," he said.

I replied. "Why would you want to do that? I'm only trying to help you and help your marriage."

He settled down and apologized.

On his fourth visit, I came into my office again, but no one was there.

Millie told me he was in there. This time I stayed in the room and called her. She said, "This better be good" and came into the room. She said, "He was here. I saw him go in."

I replied, "Now who's delusional Millie?"

She looked around and left saying, "He must really have walked out. I'll cancel him in your schedule."

I saw in small print on my calendar in my office, "Thanks Doc!" I never saw him again. Talk about the Twilight Zone … maybe my next patient will be Rod Serling or they would put me in a padded cell on Thorazine. I hardly ever drink at all, but after work, even I guzzled down a beer that day with a psychiatrist friend. I didn't tell him about anything and decided I was done helping spies, or I'd end up the patient.

I felt it was time for some major stress relief after this case and decided to fly again, gaining my pilot's license shortly after. I knew physicians who had chosen flying over golf as stress relief, or at least in addition to golf. This appeared to be a mandate for most doctors. My brother almost went pro when he graduated from medical school in 1986. I would caddy for him, but he didn't pay well.

Morning came as rapidly as my migranes, and at my desk I played solitaire. I received a phone call from who I thought was the husband of a female patient I was treating for Bipolar Disorder. I had previously consulted with her psychiatrist and recommended a medication. The psychiatrist agreed and placed her on the lowest dose. Though the medication helped, it lowered her hyper sexuality. Hyper sexuality is a possible symptom of Bipolar Disorder. Apparently in her manic phase, she was a sexual giant. Overall, between the medications and through much structured psychotherapy and subsequent testing, the psychiatrist and I were stabilizing her. The man on the phone complained her sex drive was down. This is obviously the disgruntled husband.

"She is not as intense and I don't like it," he reported.

He then insisted we take her off her medication and terminate the psychotherapy treatments. He wanted her to be a sexual beast again. Later, I confronted her on this and informed her that it would be counter-productive and unethical for the psychiatrist and I to terminate treatment, especially since she is progressing.

"That was not my husband, Doctor. You see, I have not told you everything," she said.

I stood there with my mouth open, catching more flies. Her husband didn't care less, her lover apparently did. Therapy with her just became more complicated. Nothing is ever what it seems. I found out later she had fifteen lovers. *I thought she is looking at me funny; maybe she wanted me as the sixteenth.*

Around this same time, I had begun to treat a young man who suffered from separation anxiety and a dependent personality disorder. Unfortunately, he was a chronic alcoholic as well, which was causing severe relationship issues. The psychiatrist diagnosed him with Generalized Anxiety and Bipolar Disorder. I gave him psychological tests and took an extensive history. The medication worked some. But he started using again much alcohol with Klonopin, a potentially lethal combo.

Nevertheless, he had bouts of abstinence, not atypical for alcoholics. Given his history, Mike remained sober through therapy for one year, a huge accomplishment. He eventually divorced. The divorce was hard on his eight-year-old daughter, a petite, very insightful little girl who was fully aware of her father's problem. Mike was in his early 30's when I began treating him. He was incredibly childish, caring only about sex and drinking. He drove his motorcycle at high speeds, popped wheelies, used alcohol, and found wild women willing to do anything. He was also into the S&M scene. He told me once during a therapy session that one woman put a gun to his mouth and played Russian roulette while they made love. Interesting! There were times I broke him down in therapy and he cried like a baby, talking about how much he missed his mother who died when he was a child. Mike would leave me for months at a time, but eventually showed up for a "tune-up" for a few sessions. He was with me for several years on and off, but refused to see anyone else. As if I had a premonition, I told Mike three years later during one of his guest appearances in therapy that he probably would not see his 40th birthday. I tried to shock him; he ended up shocking me. He refused inpatient treatment and work recovery. He continued to "party" with very dysfunctional women who would abuse him emotionally as he loved being dominated by them. He continued to push the limits with his motorcycle as well. When I told him what I felt, he cried out loud. I told him I hoped I scared him enough to check him in. He was not taking therapy, my suggestions, recovery or his psychiatrist seriously. That was the last time I saw him alive. Mike impacted the side of a truck with his motorcycle at a very high rate of speed three weeks later and was killed instantly, leaving his daughter to grieve alone. The young police officer who had told me this stated that it was one of the worst scenes he had ever witnessed. I told him to stop there and not tell me anymore. Grieving too, I had to take a few days off from practice to absorb this loss. I looked down at my hands and they were shaking. My body was reacting to this subconsciously. I was actually a bit traumatized. You give a man a fish, you feed him for a day, you teach a man to fish and you feed him for a lifetime. I felt I failed to teach Mike how to fish. Perhaps I just kept giving him fish in hopes he would get it. I will remember him for the rest of my life. I took this failure personally. If you stay in mental health long enough tragedy is inevitable.

I couldn't deal with Mike's death. The feeling of failure was inescapable, and his daughter was heavy on my heart. I should've saved him, right? Asking these questions that had no definitive answers made it worse. I carry responsibility in this, and I had no clue how others grew calloused to this. Maybe it's the only way to survive it.

I flew the following weekend with a friend who was a very good pilot. Needing an adrenaline rush, I told him to put it on deck as we took off. We buzzed a woman we saw hanging her laundry on a line. Although I felt we were not that low, we were low enough and she looked up. I took over and we decided to find and buzz my house. I could not have found a better way to reduce the stress than to fly with a fellow pilot on that day. We buzzed cows, horses, barns fishermen anything was fair game that day. We were on the deck. Thank goodness no one got the number on the tail. We were within FAA limits relatively speaking however. Then I powered up and headed for the clouds then took hold of God's hand for a few minutes. I returned to work thinking about how life was so fragile and how we so often take it for granted. I thought of Mike.

I returned to another colorful day at work. My office phone rang and on cue, this woman came into my office, very disheveled. Her hygiene was bad. Her breath could kill a cockroach. My Airwick failed miserably. I thought this poor woman must have been homeless for a while and her mental capacity is taxed given her obvious health problem. She was attractive, slight of build despite being on the street for so long, and very thin. Her voice sounded like she'd just inhaled helium. I began my interview, talked very slowly and started a mental health status evaluation very slowly.

I stated, "I know this might be difficult for you, but could you subtract 7 from 100, take that answer and keep subtracting it by 7 until I tell you to stop?"

She did it 10 times very rapidly and accurately. I was shocked. I thought she may have had some learning issues, only graduated from high school at best.

I told her to spell the word "world" backwards, and repeat several digits forward and backward. Again, she did this with lightning fast speed and accuracy. I think my bias was showing.

So, I asked, "By the way Clarissa, how far did you get in school? You seem, to be good with math and remembering numbers."

"I can do calculus. I'm especially good with physics and organic chemistry."

"Did you take this in high school?" I asked her.

"No, college," she replied.

"Wow, so you have some college, right?"

She laughed, "I'm graduated from medical school. I'm a doctor, a physician, or at least I used to be," she stated.

She told me to close my mouth, because my breath was bad enough and she could see my cavities. She told me to brush better, because this could cause gum issues. *Serves me right*, I thought. Again, don't judge a book by its cover. I sincerely and respectfully apologized, and promised to use Scope. After my clinical interview, I strongly encouraged her to come back to me. She was in a domestic violence situation, turned to drugs and alcohol to cope, eventually made some medical mistakes and lost her license to practice medicine. She continued her downward spiral. She claimed at one time she was a good, caring, empathetic doctor and lost her way. I so wanted so badly to work with her and help her to get back on track. I never saw her again. Yet another starfish that washed up on the beach that I couldn't throw back into the sea.

Swallowing my recent failure, I kept moving forward. I did an intake on a woman who was very depressed. She was laughing and crying at the same time. She was what we call in the profession "labile in emotions." As I so often did, I formulated possible diagnoses in my mind, Bipolar Disorder, or Schizophrenia. I tried to visualize what she told me during interview. She recently saw a young counselor who had just received her master's degree and recently passed her license exam. This counselor conducted an intake and this patient stated to her

"I'm very suicidal. I'm strongly thinking of going home now and offing myself."

The counselor replied, according to the patient, "I know, I'm writing this down."

This patient replied, "I have several means to kill myself; gun, knife and most of all, a whole bottle of Percocet (pain relievers) for my fibromyalgia pain."

The counselor apparently replied, "I got it. So what I want you to do is schedule an appointment next week, so we can begin your therapy."

The patient told me, "Was she dumb or what?"

The patient told her, "I might not be here to come back because I'll be dead."

She laughed and said "I'm in trouble if this is the best the mental health profession can do, right?"

"Wrong," I said. "You got to me and that's good. What did the therapist do next?" I asked her.

"Well, she made me an appointment to talk more about my feelings the next week."

She shook her head and cried.

I asked her, "On a 1-10 scale, 10 being the highest for "offing" yourself, where are you with that?"

She replied, "A 9 out of 10.

I said, "Why not a 10?"

She said, "There's always a chance I would botch it, you know end up a veggie tale."

I hospitalized this woman that day! I conducted several sessions with her until she improved and no further incidences occurred. During that time, I treated a person who rather would mate with his sheep than his wife and did not understand why she refused to sleep with him. I also treated a man with a diaper fetish who left me during our first few sessions because he found a perfect mate who enjoyed wearing them as well. Other cases involved getting an alcoholic airline pilot to treatment, dealing with a sadistic attorney who liked to hurt women. Getting to appropriate treatment a man who enjoyed being urinated on by ladies of the evening, to mention a few of the more interesting cases. I did talk to one of these ladies in a therapy session one time. She asked me how much I made per hour and I asked her why she wanted to know. She told me she wondered if she should become a therapist and do some good for people in a non-sexual way. I told her what I am paid per hour. She told me and I quote her directly, "That's pathetic, you are a doctor of psychology." She then went on to tell me what she made per hour and asked me to step outside to see her car. I said I could not go outside as I have patients to see, but she told me what she drove. It was a nice luxury sports car however. I told her that this was not always about the money for me. As cliché as this was I told her my joy is seeing success with the people I help. She turned and said as she was leaving, "I think I'll stay in my profession anyway. Thanks for everything Doctor."

Another once upon a time, I was treating an individual with intractable depression I will call Pete later during the day. His wife was very concerned. He looked like a zombie on a bender. He stared off into space and only mumbled. They started ECT treatment, but the psychiatrist conducting this did not communicate to the referral psychiatrist who also medicated him and they both had him on a host of medications. I called his treating referral psychiatrist informing her of med changes by the ECT psychiatrist and encouraged in a very politically polite manner, future communication. He continued his ECT (electroconvulsive shock) treatments, but he did get consent and communicated with the other doctor. They did reduce his medication and he improved.

Unfortunately, being a psychologist barred me from certain things. I called a psychiatrist four times to get him to consult with me on a case and he never called me back. Finally, I was told by his nurse/receptionist, he doesn't talk with psychologists, only other physicians. After about two weeks, I called the nurse/receptionist back telling her I was a case manager, new in the area who wanted to refer patients to him. I got a call back immediately. I told him I had a case (describing my patient he was medicating) and while I had him on the phone discussed possible medications. He said his name and mentioned he had something similar and told me the medications and doses and stated how well the patient benefited. I asked if the patient was seeing anyone for professional help, like a counselor or psychologist.

"Yes, but they are pretty useless, so I don't bother, he exclaimed calmly."

My face turned red and I was approaching stroke levels. I counted to ten, took two huge breaths.

I said in a crafty way, "Well, I know one, and mentioned my name. He is amazing and has actually helped several patients. If you ever have a chance to talk with him, he certainly stands apart from the others."

I thanked him for his courtesy and hung up. A week later, I got a call from the psychiatrist to my psychology services number. Games played on behalf of the patient are a sad affair. As Ben told me, these people are all "Seekers." I think the Army has a word for what I did, "Overcome, adapt, improvise". At least this is what my World War II Veteran father told me. He did a lot of that with my stepmother. I may have bent the rules, but I also was able to coordinate care, and get the results my patient needed.

Heading to my office one day, I was trying to talk to Jacky, my manager, but she walked away from me. I told her I wasn't done talking but she kept ignoring me and talking to everyone else. I politely waited for this conversation to end. Then I told Jacky I didn't appreciate her walking away while I was trying to converse. She looked at me as if I was a plague victim and again walked, away. I grabbed her arm, something I had never done to anyone, which pissed her off. I was angry for once however. She pulled away and told me never to touch her again. I apologized for that. I even wrote her a nice note in an apology card to her but she still disrespected me with impunity.

She yelled out loudly, "You're nothing but a spoiled brat who is a M.D. Wannabe!" I told her, "I'm a Ph.D. and that's ok with me, which is better than an office manager who is like a turbulent sea." This rhyming helped me to diffuse the situation at least for me. She gave me a dirty look and walked on.

I was incredibly frustrated at this point, but could still rhyme. I had enough, went over her head and complained to the nursing director over this unit. She admitted that one of the psychiatrists was acutely aware of how I was being treated and she vowed to keep her complaints and my complaints anonymous. She would look over what was said and act.

She told me, "If my managers and secretaries are not respecting you, then we need to talk about professionalism."

I thought, *Wow*! This is great, maybe things will change for the better. Since the psychiatrist supported me, things will now improve.

Two things happened: one is I believed the nurse manager. The second thing is I should have wished for world peace. That would have occurred faster than the changes I wanted at this mental health center at the hospital. No sooner did I get back to my office than the manager Jacky was waiting for me to ambush me.

She started, "So you went over my head. I just got a call from my boss (so much for anonymity) who stated you were bitching about us here."

I told her "Yep, and I was not the only one, so was the psychiatrist."

Both the nurse and psychiatrist clammed up, stating that I was the only one who complained... so much for loyalty. Jacky ripped me a new one and reiterated that I was nothing but a "spoiled brat M.D. Wannabe." Our nurse practitioner passed me by in the hallway about that time looking disillusioned; a huge frown on his face stating how he wanted to vaporize this hospital.

Approaching him, I said "Hey, what's happening? You look like I feel."

We talked briefly in my office and I asked him if he was experiencing some of the things I was experiencing.

"I really can't say much" as he fidgeted uncomfortably.

It was obvious I put him on the spot, so I backed off. Two days later, after he talked about what I said to his very wise wife who encouraged him to reconnect to me as I was looking for support, he knocked on my door. He apologized for "blowing me off," but wasn't sure who he could trust. He told me things that shocked me. He and two psychiatrists were the only ones' privy to see the balance sheets, even though I was on medical staff and he was not. Don't you love the mental health field? They valued his ability to write scripts and saw him as a "cash-cow." He said that they saw me only as a glorified counselor with a fictitious title of Doctor who could not write prescriptions.

Therefore, I wasn't a moneymaker. Furthermore, they only kept the mental health center open because the community wanted it, otherwise they would close it. They were all about the balance sheet at the end of the day.

"Wake up Tom," he told me. "It's business only. As a result, they didn't care if they lose you. They crunch numbers!"

"And?" I asked.

"And they haven't announced this yet, but they are downsizing me, you and the counselors and will only keep the two psychiatrists."

"I'm being downsized? I asked.

"Yep," He stated. "You went from supersize fries to half-baked little pies and everyone lies."

I added. "And we die."

"Yep, you got it."

I told him that I was thinking about putting a cockroach in Jackie's coffee.

"Good idea? I asked."

He said, "No, think bigger, a cicada!"

We laughed, "We're screwed,"

I said. "Do the counselors know?"

He said, "I only told you. They really screwed you over and because I didn't make the money they expected, they are terminating me with extreme prejudice as well. Oh the horror."

I said, "Well, I have had enough anyway. If you go, I'm done too."

We shook hands and have been friends ever since. We both resigned weeks of each other and I did not put a cicada in Jacky's coffee … because he stopped me!

Attack of the Killer Counselors
– The Correctional Center

CHAPTER FIVE

I was now out of work again and considering my options. Would I work at another hospital, mental health center or maybe a crisis center? I would probably be underpaid at a mental health center and was in crisis myself, so maybe a crisis center was not the best option. ACME Trucking was looking good when I saw an ad in the paper for a Psychologist Supervisor needed in an adolescent correctional youth services center. The pay was not great, but it was acceptable until I could find something else and it was close to my house. I interviewed for the position and was hired immediately. *Strange to be hired so quickly*, I thought.

I asked the interviewer, "How many have you interviewed so far if I might ask?" "You're the only one," she said, "and you're hired. You're perfect."

They were desperate. For some reason, they had a high turnover rate. They were having a difficult time finding someone who wanted to work in corrections; no one, save, who valued his or her life. I looked upon this as a challenge. I would be working with criminally minded and psychopathic, 12-21-year-old adjudicated felony sex offenders, oh what fun. I later found the challenge would lie not in working with the youth. The youth were a piece of cake to work with. The challenge would lie within the staff I was supervising; the "professional counseling staff" made up of three female counselors from the depths of the underworld. What a surprise. One of the counselors was very angry. She was narcissistic, wore a cropped hair cut and pointed shoes. She took any chance to defy my direction and organized the other two in attack against the new supervisor. The second woman was paranoid in personality, benign, clever, and manipulative and was subtle in how she sabotaged. I cannot count on how many times she set me up. The third woman dressed like a male, long sleeved shirt and black tie and black patent leather shoes and vest. She verbalized her anger about men in general, and, of course, me for being there. Together they would write me scathingly angry e-mails which I have kept for posterity. The three brought images of three witches crowding around a black cauldron throwing in the brew, eye of newt, tail of salamander, head of Tom, and laughing manically. *Is there anyone in the mental health field that is mentally healthy?*, I am thinking. The hits kept on coming and a colleague suggested that I pipe music into my office from KC & the Sunshine Band ..."that's the way ugh ha, ugh ha, I like it." What is it that Heath Ledger's "Joker" character stated in the film The Dark Knight, "As you know madness is like gravity...all it requires is a little push."

The psychiatrist at the facility was very healthy, and very wise. A female psychiatrist named Dr. Janice. She informed me of their personality disorders and the fact that they would tag team me to get me out of the facility.

"You see," she said turning to me, "they have not had a supervisor for over two years and have been allowed to basically do what they want. They are very pathological and cunning probably can't get a job anywhere else, and, of course, dislike you."

I said, "Why me? I'm new, what did I do?"

"You exist and you're a male. You probably have a good lawsuit for discrimination probably, but since you are a supervisor it may be hard to prove. The thing is, you have to get tough with them. Also, if you do, however, no one in the higher administration will support you because they fear the union, so you're kind've screwed."

I decided I would treat them with kindness. Big mistake! I tried that before in the past and you would think I would learn. What was it Ben tried to teach me about potholes?

These ladies didn't mess around. They were good. The nicer I was the meaner they got. I encouraged them and signed off on reports but their rage intensified. I was taught to respect women, so I stayed soft on them. They attacked me verbally in front of others. There were perpetual scathing e-mail attacks. They blamed me for things I had no idea or input about. I was stabbed in the back and everything I said was negatively twisted. They were the incarnate of evil and they acted in concert to drive me out. On more than one occasion, I felt there was a parallel process occurring. Many of these adolescent youths were abused in their childhoods and, unfortunately, by the staff as well. Cover-ups were the norm at this facility. By societal standards, these were throw-away kids. A meeting was called concerning a plan for a youth but it went south and ultimately made things worse. I was blamed by one of the counselors for the faulty plan. Later, they found out I wasn't even in the room for that meeting, nor was I trained to write a plan to assist in that meeting.

Similarly, since I was new to the facility and had not been trained on agency procedures, I asked one of the counselors on the procedure in formulating a suicide prevention plan. This counselor refused to help me and I did the best I could in designing one. She didn't tell me there was a standard template I could've used and made me present my draft to the group. I confronted her about it but it didn't matter.

She stated, "Do what. I don't know what you mean."

Angrily, I said, "You darn well do, and next time, I'll write you up."

She complained to the union that I singled her out for harassment, and she filed a grievance against me. I informed my supervisor that something had to change and I would need to go up to a higher level to remedy this situation. My supervisor told me to leave things alone because politics played too large a role in this. I wasn't sure if she said this because it was true, or because she did not want to make any waves, a tsunami perhaps. In the meantime, the scathing e-mails continued and these women continued to defy me and my directives. Worried about the care the youthful offenders were receiving, I lost 20 pounds in this job and was not sleeping well. I continued to try to work with the kids, teaching coping skills, anger management, and relaxation techniques. I was told by a dear friend who now holds an MBA, that the children responded well to me and I had a positive impact on at least two of the youth. One was discharged back to his home. I wanted to teach some of the kid's magic tricks, but any tricks or kits I might need to bring into the facility would be considered contraband and I would have been investigated. I did show them the disappearing quarter trick; a slight of hand trick. The problem is that one of the kids absconded with the quarter so that it could not reappear. It had permanently disappeared. I then thought *if I could make a quarter disappear, could I make three angry women disappear*? Just a thought!

The frightening part for me was that these counselors were under my license and ultimately, I would be responsible if something they did harmed a youth. On another occasion, a child threatened suicide and one of the counselors decided to leave the facility without addressing the problem. The child was automatically locked in a special, barren room until morning placed in a suicide typed body bag where arm and leg movement was limited. I was again, frustrated because this child could have been assessed and a plan developed if this counselor would have done her job. She was written up by a manager and I supported the write-up. Thus, the three counselors escalated their attacks, chanting Kill Dr. Tom, Kill Dr. Tom. Then two events lead to my thinking that this job would not work out. The first was that when in a library writing notes a youth inmate snuck in, and was having an affair with another youth, who he found out was cheating on him with yet another youth. This first youth came into the library and I did not notice him. A loud crash occurred as this youth put his arm through a glass that was interfaced with wire mesh, and as he pulled his arm out he shredded it. He expressed his anger through self-mutilation. It looked like hamburger and he must have hit the brachial artery as blood spurted out all over. Before I could react, the correctional officers were on it and put towels on his arm and called an alert and 911. Blood was everywhere and frightened me. His arm skin was hanging down and his screams were horrific. Nurses were on the spot immediately. He was life flighted out of the facility. I was visibly shaken by this, even though I saw it from a distance. I looked pale by one nurse's assessment. She told me she would write me off the rest of the day, as being sick, I was later admonished by the facility director for not alerting him as to my departure. I left and went to bed. Then a mouse that I fed cheese from my sandwich was killed when a woman screamed when she saw it on my desk. I befriended this mouse some time back when it had the courage to come out of its hole in my office. I threw crumbs of cheese out and it became braver and I soon conditioned it to come out as it was looking for food. When I came back to my office a janitor told me not to worry as he killed it. Again, I felt sorrow for that baby mouse. I thought "Oh, the horror, the horror." Everywhere, I seemed to encounter human frailty, fear or some form of projected anger.

I knew now what a wounded, bleeding fish felt like alone in the ocean waiting for the great white shark to come and eat him. I had three white sharks circling me. They complained behind my back to my supervisor that I wasn't carrying my weight and was not providing adequate supervision. A supervisor is only as good as the system is around him or her that provides support. In my case, my system only wanted to cover its' own butt. No one wanted to challenge these counselors or their union and I was offered up as the lamb for slaughter. After almost a year, I decided to pull myself off the cross and resign, much to the women's great delight. I'm sure they were doing a victory dance around their cauldron. There was no fanfare as I left the facility. I was told I had a positive impact on some of the kids and on some of the staff who very much enjoyed me being there. I felt humbled, humiliated, but perhaps a bit wiser. I was saddened knowing that care and treatment for these youths could have been so much better. Someday if I would ever have the money I would love to have built a camp for these kids.

I was brought up by my father to nurture, love, revere women. I never felt the sting of a woman so much as the time I worked in corrections and had to "supervise" three of them. These were very angry, hurt women who, unfortunately, were counseling male youth sex offenders – go figure. Hurt people hurt people. There is truth to the notion that hell hath no fury like a woman scorned, or in my case, three.

Just when I was thinking that I am the bane of displeasure for women, a very nice lady at a Tim Horton's restaurant bought me a cup of coffee. She was a stranger. I told her thank you, but did not understand why she did that. She told me for two reasons: the first being that she is paying it forward. I asked so what is the second reason? She stated flatly, because if anyone looks like they need it you certainly do. She and I laughed and I returned the favor and bought her a doughnut. She thanked me and told me to take care of myself and smiled at me as she left. This was therapeutic for me that day and reaffirmed my faith in women.

PRIVATE PRACTICE

CHAPTER SIX

Out of work again, I took two weeks off before looking again for another position. Mentally and physically exhausted, I felt like a dried-out herring. It was me against the mental health system and the system was winning. Just as I was preparing for Hari Kari, I received a call from a female psychologist who I had known briefly from my days as a rehabilitation psychology supervisor. She was a devout Christian counselor, went to church every Sunday and read passages from the Bible. She somehow knew that I was out of a job and offered me a position with her in her private practice. I do believe there is something to be said for paranoia at this point, and later I found she had an agenda. I was part of her plan to essentially increase her wealth at my expense. It was like the old sideshow barkers saying "Heads I win, tails, you lose" as they toss the coin up.

She confessed she felt I was a very "introspective and talented psychologist and the practice would benefit from having me".

This was a trick statement. On one hand, she complemented me, but on the other hand, used me. I gave her my heartfelt work, taught her things she didn't realize and increased her knowledge about testing, psychopathology and strategies for counseling. In the meantime, I was seeing 35 to 40 patients per week, which was a lot to keep straight, and making around five hundred dollars per month. Something was not equitable here. I found out later from some of her patients that she would take them to church on Sunday and charge them. She would also sleep during sessions and bend the ethical code so many times that I think she fractured it. When she worked group therapy with sex offenders proclaiming cure-alls, she was challenged by one who called the State in. She immediately researched methods that help for offenders who participate in group and put it in manual form. She showed this to the State who backed off. They never questioned why she ran groups for sex offenders especially on Halloween night. They thought she was doing the community a service by keeping them off the street, where in truth although this was in part laudable, the hidden agenda was that she could charge the state a good amount of money to bring her as many as they could. She cleaned up that night.

She gave me a female patient who in her eyes was too challenging. When she found out her insurance was very good and paid well, coupled with the fact that this patient merely had minor adjustment problems to her career path, she convinced this patient to come with her instead of me. I started to get it. The piano finally fell on me. I told her the 70/30 split where I get 70 percent and she gets 30 percent seemed to be the reverse. I'm just saying. She had some medical and physical health problems and despite the way she interpreted her "Christian" philosophy, my heart ached for her. The money didn't mean as much to me and despite what she had done to me and her patients, not to say that she did not do some good for some people – she had, I essentially felt sorry for her. She was in and out of hospitals so many times, I couldn't swallow the truth: her body had had enough. I visited her as often as I could and tried to support her emotionally. The last time I saw her she told me she was going home and thanked me for being a good man and even greater psychologist. She encouraged me not to stop believing in myself or God, even when it seemed at times I was forsaken, which it seemed was a lot. The following week, she passed away, but I never forgot her words, forgave her and hoped that God would welcome her with open arms. Her family wanted to take me to court because they felt I owed their mother money for practicing with her. My wife threatened to bring in an auditor and they paid me some of the money they felt was owed to me, and dropped the suit. It was not about the money. I just wanted peace from this profession. I held no grudge to her. Life is about movement, and problems result from being stuck.

A few days later, I rented a brand-new Cessna 172 aircraft with the latest avionics and flew to an airport where a lake was. I sat by myself and just grieved for her, my patients and even myself. I felt alone and humbled. I pondered whether this profession was for me or not. I tried to be my own shrink and used self-talk. Eleanor Roosevelt said, "Courage comes from doing courageous things."

I thought, *I'm either crazy or very courageous for continuing to be beaten up by a profession that was supposed to be so caring and humanistic.* This is not to say that there are not great people in this profession who care and help people – they do. I've met some. They do exist. When you find them, like Ben, they are a joy to behold. However, I kept on questioning and questioning. I sat there alone watching baby ducks with their mother waddling along sort of what I am doing in the mental health field. As the sun started to set I climbed back into the cockpit, did my pre-flight check, started the engine and took off back to my home airport. The flight back was quiet and peaceful, and the setting sun made it more beautiful. I landed alone with no one around, parked the aircraft and went home less stressed that night.

MINDING MY OWN BUSINESS

CHAPTER SEVEN

After careful thought and weeks of getting beyond myself and my instinctual need to work for others, I decided to take out a loan and start my own business. Yes, I had thought about Acme Trucking or being a short-order cook, but still had a huge amount to pay on my student loan. I figured I might as well keep trying to make my degree pay for itself and make a difference in someone's life. Besides, I felt now like a Timex watch. I took a licking, but kept on ticking. I also started to read books on assertiveness and took a seminar on it. You would think that being a psychologist I'd know all that stuff. I probably did, but had difficulty applying it to myself.

It reminded me of a cardiologist I once knew. He was extremely overweight, breathed very hard walking upstairs. He smoked cigarettes like they were candy. He looked like a battered freight train, yet had the audacity to tell me to always exercise and never smoke as this would "weaken your health, young man." I went to his funeral the following year. I always wondered what killed him. We in health care do not self-care.

I started to put walls up, not emotional walls, real ones. I even painted the walls and moved in furniture. Again, I reminded myself that this was a good thing, even though I would be looking. I'd be looking poverty in the face if my business failed.

If that happened, and that was highly likely, I would probably wonder if I would be a stunt double in Hollywood for Tom Cruise – Ha!

My wife has good business sense and is intelligent, I know this because I tested her IQ, but her personality is a bit stronger than mine. I should have tested that too. She told me if she supervised the counselors at the correctional facility, they would not have breathed wrong without consequences. She has had organizational management training and has been a manager of a wing at a hospital. In my estimation, she can come across as a bit too Attila the Hunnish, however, she was right. She would have put those lassies in their places, I'm convinced of that, and would have relished the idea of going into battle with the union with her at my side. She was very supportive.

Years ago, my wife had taken and scored well on the MCAT (Medical College Admissions Test) and was accepted to medical school, but didn't go. After watching her father suffer endless pain and obstacles from being on life support himself, she was forced to decide, along with the rest of the family, whether to turn it off. They chose to give him peace and shut it off. It was one of the hardest tragedies she ever had to face. After watching her father and family suffer like that, she couldn't find it in her to support the same experience possibly happening to others in that situation.

She is excellent at what she does. She bosses around adolescents in her library as she is now a high school librarian. This deflects the heat off me as well. *Better them than me,* I think. She has a master's degree in computer science. This book is a result of her helping me write it on the computer, and my father constantly encouraging me to write it. I stink with computers. I know they have it in for me-no really! I can almost hear my computer talk to me when I get on it. "Hello Tom, I'm your computer and I'm here to mess your life up again, Moooohaaaaaaa." Well I would like to see the computer play golf.

Nevertheless, she also helped with the ergonomics of the facility. She painted, or actually I painted, the earth tones for the office. Since that time, I was complemented on how the office looks. I tried to keep the office relaxing. I wanted my office staff to be caring, encouraging and respectful. Things I generally did not always find in the mental health field myself. What a concept, right? I was so naïve.

I think I should have given all my staff the MMPI-2 test, a personality test which screens for pathology. Again, on the surface, people come across as relatively balanced until you get to know them. It's like that honeymoon period when you're dating and five months later, you realize you're engaged to a werewolf and she or he howls at the full moon. Now you got problems.

I was invited out to the hospital in another town on a Saturday per a patient of mine. She cleared it with the unit psychiatrist and the group itself. He was tall, a very good looking middle-aged man, but seemed insensitive as all get out. Usually, you do not see too many psychiatrists run group therapy sessions; at least I didn't. I was looking forward to learning from this man and perhaps contributing something myself. It was a group of women who suffered domestic violence issues. I thought this group might benefit from a female therapist; however, if they accepted a male, maybe it was to show them what a "healthy male" looked like; sort of modeling, if you will. As the group started, I was introduced as another doctor, a clinical psychologist. Despite my previous encounters with angry women in my past, I remained respectful, professional and very supportive overall. I basically validated and reflected their feelings back. I mainly listened and empathized with them. The psychiatrist started off well, and even provided insight to their feelings. I was impressed. Things appeared to be going well. Then one especially angry woman seemed to challenge the psychiatrist on a point. He seemed a bit irritated. She pressed her point. That's when things got especially ugly. He retorted back, "Your especially intensive anger obviously relates directly to your time of the month." I'm being kind. He stated this much differently. I turned to look at him in utter shock. When I did, he was attacked and taken off his chair by this woman as if tackled like a football player. He was on his chair one minute; the next it was empty. I looked at the other women who now joined her comrade in the attack. Now, I believe I leaked in my pants, thinking I was their next victim and took refuge behind a piano that was in the room. Soon, nurses, orderlies and security broke the fray apart. The doctor went to the ER. The ladies later stated they felt I was supportive and empathic, thus I warranted no reprisal. I would rather face a raging-bull-elephant. I learned some things from this venture one being to never, never talk about a woman's cycle in a negative manner. Never discuss it at all. Secondly, try real hard not to tick off a band of angry women. I visited the doctor later while he was still bandaged and told him thanks for the experience. It was a valuable learning experience. Maybe we could do it again sometime —not!

I started to advertise my new business at the local movie theatre. I was in the film club in college and made both 16 mm films and eight mm films, so I felt the visual media was the way to go. I created short-film ads in-between features. I walked the streets placing flyers at local businesses, hospitals, attorney's offices, CPA's, everyone I could think of. I took out a billboard ad, fortunately without my face on it. I took out ads for my business in the local paper and outside of my town. I also hired secretaries, two of which I treated very well, but did not provide enough structure and they exercised their "free will" behind my back. One of which exercised her free will to point out things that needed improving in my practice to other therapists. This was bad press that I didn't need. Another did the most minimal work, wrote scathing letters to patients and other professional companies concerning services she felt we were not providing. This was done all behind my back, of course, even signing my name to documents without my knowledge. I only found out because one company wanted to sue me back. I didn't know I was suing them in the first place. I pampered the ladies, gave them increases in salaries for less than a year's work, bought those individuals gifts but didn't provide them with the structure they needed.

Everything you should not do in business, I managed to do. I was lucky I did not go bankrupt my first year. Finally, I hired a business consultant who re-organized me as well as the business. He taught me to set goals and expectations for me, the staff and the business in general. One of my "former" secretaries got into a conflict with my partner who had another consultation company with me. She left abruptly in a huff; some of my patients saw this and left vowing not to return. Of course, what do I do, plead with her to come back – huge mistake. I had to let her go a few weeks after anyway when I found her e-mailing family members that I was too easy and associated myself with the rear end of horses in terms of staff. Yea, I'm a business man.

Anyway, long story short, I was determined to make the business work despite me. I was going to capitalize on my strengths and hire people around me who had strength in areas I was weak. This worked and the business started to flourish. I started hiring counselors, physicians, intake coordinators, billing people and marketing people. I was expanding and best of all, I was the boss. I found myself not being abused anymore except by myself. I was harder on myself than anyone I worked for. Something was wrong with this. I was now beating myself up. I was driving myself hard. My new secretary said I looked like "yesterday's road kill," but she still loved me. Hum!

As I drove home, I had an especially hard day, even my intern that I was supervising complained that I was not available enough because of my working so hard. I must have rolled slowly through a stop sign, because I was stopped by a lady patrol officer. As she pulled me over, I watched her in the rear-view mirror.

I said, "Why, hello officer."

She said, "May I see your driver's license please?"

I said "Yes, ma'am," as I pulled my license out and handed it to her.

She looked at it then looked at me and gave it back.

"Are you aware you rolled through that last stop sign Sir?"

I was thinking *if I was aware, I probably would not have done it.*

I said, "No ma'am."

She said, "Well, I'm only going to give you a verbal warning. Please take your time and come to a full stop, ok?"

I said, "Yes Ma'am. Thank you."

She said, "Have a nice day, Sir."

As she walked back to her car, I called out, "Ma'am!"

She came back and said, "Sir?"

"Could you do me a favor?" I stated.

"Favor, Sir?" She replied.

"Yes, Could you please withdraw your firearm and shoot me," I said.

"What?" she replied with a concerned affect.

"Shoot me," I said. "Please."

She looked at me strangely and said, "I could not do that, Sir. You pose no threat to me. Why do you wish me to shoot you?" she replied.

"My profession is getting to me," I said.

"Well then, you probably need to see a psychologist, Sir," she said back.

I replied, "I am a psychologist. Thanks anyway."

I drove away with her standing there looking at me puzzled. Sometimes you have to make life fun or funny or you go crazy. Humor is good medicine. Phyllis Diller was reported to have said, "A smile on your face is a curve that sets things straight," or something like that.

When I got home, I put my head in a bucket of ice water. My wife wanted to call 911 and commit me to my former psych unit. I told her even the police didn't want to kill me today. I told her I was just bringing myself back to reality. Even our dog Buddy, a Beagle, looked at me weird and turned its' head. I told Buddy, quit looking at me like that or I'll put you on an extra dose of Viagra, then take away all potential mates. Buddy put his head down and walked away depressed, apparently. He was an incredibly horny dog. Where he went at nights I never knew. All I knew is there seemed to be a lot more Beagle pups in the neighborhood. Sometime later Buddy was shot and killed by someone. When I called the sheriff, they told me, "It's only a dog. You will get over it. Get yourself a new one." *So much empathy and too little time* I thought. I buried him with full military honors. One of my patients felt bad for me and wanted to give me a horse. It was a kind gesture but not the same. It probably could not jump on my lap like buddy did.

The next day, I was introduced to a young woman who had seen a social worker for several years without any marked results. She saw my ad in the paper and decided to give me a try, mostly because I took her insurance, which was, of course, one of the lowest paid to professionals. I conducted my interview, which was interesting since I encountered two different personalities from the get go. I'm thinking, do I do two different interviews? I start talking with "alters." Now, I know mental health professionals are divided on whether Multiple Personality Disorder, now called Dissociative Identity Disorder, truly exists. Dr. Cornelia Wilbur, a psychiatrist who treated Sybil, apparently believed it, wrote several articles on it, and accepted it as a genuine disorder. Other doctors, social workers, counselors and psychologists debunked it. Whether I believed it wasn't as important as the patient believing it, and I went with the flow. I researched the disorder that night, looking at journal articles, symptoms and treatment strategies. She was textbook, or maybe read the textbook herself. Who knows? As I'm talking with her, another "alter" comes out, all women. One was seductive. I found that alter interesting, the other was manly, the other was a protector and the other was acting as a punisher and she labeled that one as such. She was aware of three of them. I pointed out the last one. After a few sessions, I told his lady I would refer her to a specialist who works with dissociative disorders. She stated, "You are the chosen one and I know you will be able to help me." I'm thinking, so what alter or personality chose me? We discussed past issues of trauma and her "protector" spoke of the abuse (rape) she suffered repeatedly as a child by a cousin. Her family refused to believe it, punished her for lying. She was only 9 years old. Psychological testing revealed a Borderline Personality Disorder within a Paranoid Delusional System and/or Dissociative Disorder. She had been in and out of psychiatric hospitals for most of her adult life and I'm thinking she could be faking this because she was "institutionalized" so much and learned from the various systems she was in. Annie, as I'll call her, felt very comfortable with me, but she decided to test me one day. It seems her previous therapist would chase her if she threatened to cut herself and would show her "razor blades," and proceed to cut on herself. While Annie was laughing, the therapist would run after her. It became a game of avoidance and distraction. In the meantime, I consulted a therapist who was an expert on these disorders and encouraged me to keep treating her with her guidance. So, I did.

I told Annie up front "If you cut and run, I'm not chasing you, not even for fun".

She decided to put me to the test, brought in blades and cut very superficially. When I moved to stop this, she ran out my door. I called the police. They asked me what I wanted done. I told them to take her to the hospital and have an attending look at her and evaluate her for the Psych Unit. By the way, show them the razor blades you took off her.

I never had that problem again. I researched again more on multiple personality disorders. I referred her to a physician who felt she was malingering, but put her on Topamax nevertheless. I worked very hard with her toward "integration of her personality." Then the insurance company called my office. She was having a breakdown and needed to see me, they pleaded. We will pay you triple your rate to see her. I asked, "Is she suicidal?" They said no, but she is very distressed. I told the insurance company to call the police or fire department ambulance and/or get her husband to take her to the ER at the hospital to evaluate her. Again, they pleaded with me and again offered triple my usual rate per hour. I reluctantly conceded. Their persistence pushed me to cave against my better judgment.

As Annie came in, she looked like a train wreck. She was completely disheveled, appeared almost psychotic. I didn't know how she even drove to my office even though she only lived a few blocks away. I put her on my couch and attempted to talk with her. I had my door open, but my secretary had just left. All the signs were there. I had a bad feeling, however. Just then, I got a call, like an idiot, turned my back to get the phone (as if I didn't know better). It was her husband calling to make sure she had got there alright. I told him she doesn't look well. She's almost catatonic. I strongly encouraged him to come and take her to the hospital. As I turned around, she had a sardonic smile on her face, something you see in horror films, pulled out a razor blade faster than Billy the Kid could pull out a six gun, and proceeded to cut her wrists, while staring at me. Blood shot out everywhere. I was horrified and leapt at her; she struck out at me, nicking me in the throat. I grabbed her arm, we wrestled on the ground and I got a call from my business partner. While holding her down with my legs and arm, I answered the phone very calmly, "Hi, I'm a little tied up right now. Can I give you a call back? Thanks. Talk with you in a bit, ok? Bye." With that, she kneed me in the private area, which really hurt, laughed and stepped on me jumping over me, I can't remember as I was almost comatose and ran bleeding all over my new carpet toward the door. I vaguely heard and through blurry eyes saw her husband come through the door tackling her yelling, "I got her Doc, don't worry." She tried to cut him, but he got the blades away, of which she had two. I crawled to my phone and called 911, explaining what had happened while holding my crotch and gasping for breath. It seemed like the whole SWAT team came. At least seven officers came in, jumped on her, and then, when the "situation was contained" per one officer, they motioned for the paramedics to come in. They bandaged her up, tethered her to a gurney and sent her to the hospital. Finally, one paramedic who knew me came back to my office.

"You ok, Doc? Doc? Doc?"

Finally, I snapped out of it then I said, "Peachy keen, never felt better."

He noticed a small cut on my neck and said, "Let me patch that up and give you a tetanus shot."

"Give me a distemper shot as well," I replied.

He laughed, "That's one thing I like about you, Doc. even when you're bleeding, and you still have a sense of humor."

She later stabilized and went on to college. Annie told me thanks for helping her and was sorry for what she put me through. I told her thanks back…for not killing me, and we both laughed. I never saw her again.

The next day, I was assaulted two more times. One from the insurance company who stated they couldn't pay me the rate offered me for seeing Annie because they didn't send me a confirmed "in writing" agreement. I got less than my one hour regular fee and also would not pay me for prior testing I had done on her because the authorization was two days late and they refused to back date it. I was screwed again, naturally.

Then a little boy came in with his mother. He was dressed as an Indian. It seems he liked to play cowboys and Indians. He had a bow and arrow with a rubber tip. He had ADHD and ODD (Oppositional Defiant Disorder). His mother set no limits with him and he seemed like a monkey on meth amphetamine; he was everywhere, like I was watching a sped-up film reel. He was there then not there. I swear he was a blur when he moved. When I asked him to settle down a bit and go by his mother, he shot me in the head with an arrow, which stuck to my upper forehead. It had superglue, I swear. I had to walk past my other patients and secretary with an arrow stuck to my head. I told my secretary to stop laughing and help me pull this "infernal Satan's play thing" off me.

As she pulled, she said, "Wow, the suction on this sucker, it's like a leech on steroids." She finally pulled it off, leaving a red circle on my forehead and her shoeprint on my chest. The next day a deaf woman came in with her interpreter. She was talking about being violated by her boyfriend and talked about the abuse. The interpreter asked me if she should tell me everything she says, and what I say.

I said, "Of course."

This was a bit too literal however; as I thought she would be more discriminating. When I heard of the abuse, I said, "Oh shit!" because it sounded horrific. Then the interpreter signed this exactly, and the deaf woman said back, "I'm a Christian and I do not like foul language."

To which I replied to the interpreter "You told her I said, Oh shit?"

She then told her that I questioned this.

I said in exasperation, "No! Stop signing. Just tell her the nice things don't tell her shit," I said.

Then I asked when was the last time she was hurt by this guy, and the interpreter told her "He does seemingly not believe you were injured, he won't tell you shit."

She was outraged.

I asked the interpreter – "Ok, what did you tell her now?"

I inferred that you were in disbelief. I told her don't do this, I believe her. All I want to do is know if she is in current harm.

She told me "Well she won't tell you shit now."

I told the interpreter, "Where did you go to sign language school?"

Then more signing, then the deaf lady suddenly gets up and slaps me and leaves.

The interpreter than said, "She told me she is not going to take your shit anymore, and is leaving."

I'm thinking *ok –what just happened? I think I will take up sign language myself now.*

Then I shrugged this off and went on to the next patient! This patient suffered from some vague visual hallucinations, but could tell me, "There's a red spot or circle on your head, doctor."

I responded quickly with, "No Martha, you're obviously hallucinating again."

I referred her to our physician for a medication evaluation. In the meantime, I wore a baseball cap from the Chicago cubs, the rest of the day.

The following week, I had a friend from Chicago call me on my cell phone wanting some advice concerning her husband. Well, this was weird. She had the same first name as a patient of mine. My patient had somehow managed to get my cell number and I thought she was my friend from Chicago calling. I was driving back from lunch. My patient was waiting for me outside my office in her car when she called. Again, I thought it was my friend from Chicago. The conversation went something like this as I remember.

I said, "Hi Jan, how are you?"

"I'm fine, Doc. I'm waiting for you," she replied.

I said, "Hey, we're friends. You don't have to call me Doc and what do you mean you're waiting for me?"

She said, "What – what do you mean?"

I said, "Well, you're not my patient."

She said, "Yes I am!"

I replied, "No you're not. You may need some advice or suggestions, but it's not like you're my patient. We're friends, ok?"

She said, "No, we're not, you're my doctor, my psychologist."

I said, "Jan, stop this. I'm not your psychologist, I'm a friend. What's wrong with you?" She said, "Doc, are you ok? Please, I'm waiting outside your office."

I stated, "Did you fly in from Chicago? How do you know where my office is?"

She said, "Doctor Tom, I have never been to Chicago and I'm at your office waiting."

I said, "You grew up there. What's going on with you, Jan?"

She said, "Just come to your office."

It was Jan, my patient and I said, "Oh it's you, Jan."

She said, "And is there any other Jan?"

I replied, "I'll tell you all about it inside."

Jan said, "I think you need a shrink yourself, Doc."

I had a bad case of the stupid's that day.

The following week, two incidences occurred which tended to change my view on how I looked at people. The first was an ex policeman who came to me for an alcohol evaluation.

As I started the evaluation, he suddenly interrupted and stood up stating, "Oh! Hey Doc, I just thought of something. Have you ever seen a bullet wound?"

I started to say, "As a matter of fact, I ..."- but didn't finish my statement. He turned around, pulled his pants down to my unbelievable surprise and pointed to the top of his left cheek, and then suddenly, a large sound, which seemed to rock my office, came out.

"Sorry Doc, Did I get you? Must have been the beans I had for lunch."

The blast was fierce and knocked me back almost off my chair. I reeled in both panic and disgust.

He pulled up his pants and replied, "Did you see the hole, Doc?"

The air was thick. I could barely see my own hand. We eventually finished the evaluation and I transferred him to a drug and alcohol recovery center in town for treatment for both alcohol and gas. I then looked up and saw a fly explode in a fiery ball as it flew through the office. It saluted me as it spiraled down in flames. A fellow aviator bit the dust.

The following day, I was asked to perform a psychological evaluation for a gastric-bypass candidate. I had just, bought about three weeks ago, a beautiful recliner. It was large, soft and very comfortable. I enjoyed, after hours kicking back in it, listening to soft music and unwinding after a difficult day. It was my pride and joy. I went to a furniture store and I knew the guy who owned it. I treated his son a year earlier for depression and now his son was in college, had a girlfriend and was doing very well. The only problem was he wanted to become a psychologist. Oh well. Nevertheless, his father was so appreciative that he gave me the chair at cost despite my insistence that the insurance company paid me for helping his son. He said, "Dr. Tom let's face it, they don't even pay you half of what you're worth."

Well true as that may be, I honestly couldn't take it for cost. Before I could argue any further, he and his crew had already loaded it in my SUV and I paid cost. I thanked him with my beautiful new chair in tow.

Then … disaster struck in the form of Mr. Jones. Mr. Jones came into my office walking with two canes, one in each hand. He was friendly and cooperative, but possibly one of the largest human beings I had ever laid eyes on. He was massive. I did not have a chair large enough except; however, my new recliner. He weighed around four hundred and ninety pounds, close to a quarter of a ton of human being. Frankly, I was stunned he was still alive. His wife was both upset and frightened for him and so was I. He had a host of medical problems including diabetes and had undergone a heart bypass, amazingly. His doctor told him if he didn't lose weight, he would probably die within a year. He had lost weight in the past, especially after surgery, but gained it back and then some. He looked at my new recliner. I immediately knew what he was thinking.

"No, No, Mr. Jones, not there," I shouted out loud in protest.

"Well, where then?" he said without hesitation and in a frustrated tone. I did not have a chair large enough. Suddenly there was a knock on my door. It was my secretary who motioned me outside.

"Where are you going to put him?" she said in a panicked voice.

"I don't know. He wants to sit in my recliner," I stated with desperation.

"Will it hold him?" She replied.

"I don't know if it can hold nearly a quarter of a ton," I replied.

"We are not equipped for this problem," she said.

"You think?" I replied in exasperation and with sarcasm. I went back in only to see Mr. Jones in my recliner and I said a quick "recliner prayer." I started my evaluation and outlined my procedure. I heard a cry of help, a low moan coming from my chair. It was squeaking under the weight. Slowly, it started to list to port. I'm thinking, *oh, please hold, please hold*. I prayed to the God of all Recliners. Suddenly, with a crash, the left side gave way. I thought of Quint in the film *Jaws*, yelling out to the transom, "it's giving way" and with a thud, he and the chair went to the ground. My greatest fear was realized. I was frozen with shock and fearful for him.

He shouted out, "I'm ok, I'm ok, but your chair is dead, I'm afraid."

I helped him up and told him how worried I was that he might have gotten hurt. I would have to reschedule the appointment until I could get a bigger boat, I mean, more solid chair. He took it in good spirits, apologized again, and slowly left my facility. I walked over to my desk drawer, taking a small Nerf gun out with Nerf darts. I have toys in my room for when I work with children. Just then, my secretary came in with tears in her eyes.

"That was your favorite chair too," she stated in a caring and remorseful tone.

I did not say a word, heard a final dying squeak from my chair, walked up to the chair, pointed the Nerf gun at it and shot it. I had to put it down. I was depressed the rest of the day. But I was glad Mr. Jones was not hurt that was my real concern. The chair was dead. I could replace the chair. But I could not replace Mrs. Jones.

My secretary likes animals and her office was by a bay window, and at night we would see raccoons come around out of the woods. When she would go home I would tell her the next day that the raccoon family came by, tapped on the window and was asking for her. She would say that's impossible, like what would they say?

I told them "Well, the baby of the group misses you and tells me when you are not here." "Well Tom, where is she?", he stated to me.

To which I reply "She went home guys to her family but she will be back tomorrow."

I tell my secretary "They all go home with their tails between their legs and their heads down because they miss you."

She tells me, "You know that's touching, I almost can see this and believe you."

I said, "Well you heard of Alvin and the chipmunks, right? So where is the problem here?"

She then looks at me and says, "One of us needs serious help and it's not me."

The following day, I was driving to work and as I came to a fork in the road, no I did not see Bigfoot, I saw a woman driver in a van pull up on the other side. We both stopped at our stop signs, but I reached mine first. Despite this, I motioned for her to go ahead. She did not move, so I started to go. As I went along, I noticed her coming up fast behind me, tail-gaiting me and cursing at me, giving me a not so nice hand (or finger) gesture. I wasn't sure what this was all about, as she weaved in and out of traffic at amazing speeds to catch up with me. I thought, *ok, why me?* I couldn't drive and get her license number at the same time, but saw the police station and pulled in front. She pulled alongside of me declaring I was a traffic menace. She yelled obscenities at me and did not allow her to go first at the stop sign, given she was a lady. She saw a police officer come out of the building and sped away. I decided good or bad, just to leave well enough alone and went along to my practice. When I got there, I noticed a van like the one that assaulted me, but threw it to coincidence. *I mean there are hundreds of vans that look like hers,* I thought. *What are the chances I got the same Paranoid Delusional Stalker, right?*

As I came in, my secretary stated, "We got a winner here, and she's angry. She said some jerk wouldn't let her go first from the stop sign and sped away."

I looked through the glass at the lady filling out the forms. Yep, you guessed it. My luck, it was my angry Paranoid Delusional Road Stalker. Lucky me! When the secretary called her to say Dr. Tom will see you now, you should have seen her face. You should have seen my face. Yep, I'm the jerk, I reported to my secretary. She looked at me with a puzzled face.

I said, "Hi and how you are today? Let me guess, angry a bit?"

"So you're the A-hole who didn't let me go first off that stop sign," she said.

I said, "It's Dr. A-hole and your name is Grace, right? Hmmm, interesting! I mean, it doesn't seem you're living up to your name."

"What does that mean," she replied with mounting frustration.

"Never mind," I said, "You've got a bigger problem."

As I looked over her paperwork, I said, "It seems here that you are court-ordered to me for a psychological evaluation and recommendations as to an anger management program. Says furthermore," I stated, "that you have alcohol issues, a domestic violence charge against you for assaulting your husband and kicking his dog."

"It's my dog too," she replied angrily.

"Well, Grace," I said, "you must comply with me and this court order because if you don't, I tell the courts and its' pass no go time. I mean, you go to jail and perhaps you might find a girlfriend to abuse."

Suddenly, Grace's attitude changed. She came in like a lion, and went out like a lamb. "You have that power, Dr. Tom?" she said more meekly.

"Ah! Yea Grace, I do," I said slyly. "So, what's it going be, Ms. Grace? You going to go peaceful and comply with me, or do I have Acme Trucking impound your vehicle? Because your new hotel reservations will be at Penn State."

"You win Doctor. I'm sorry," she said.

I had no problem after that with Grace.

My secretary said, "Wow, Dr. Tom, you certainly have a way with women!"

"I always thought that too," I said.

"What did you do?" she replied.

"I gave her an offer she couldn't refuse," in my best Marlon Brando voice.

She said, "Your next patient is here, oh Godfather," as she slapped another chart to my chest.

I was asked to go on the radio a few times and talk about a variety of topics: depression during the holidays, coping with stressful times, the joys and tragedy of bipolar disorder, working with angry women who are road stalkers etc. However, when I'm on the radio, I love to joke around, use humorous anecdotes at times to liven up the discussion and help people not take life too seriously. I had a perfectionist call in one time and he couldn't forgive himself for not getting straight A's. He had all A's and one B+ on his college report card in a term. He should have seen my grades. He would have freaked out. He was deeply religious.

I said, "What do you think God might say? If he is merciful, wouldn't he forgive you?" "He would, but I can't forgive myself," he replied.

Then I remembered what my professor at school taught me to say in situations like this.

I replied, "It's so sad."

"What's so sad?" he said.

"Oh! That you have higher standards than God and he has such low standards." He didn't reply.

In another instance, a guy and his wife kept going to church and praying they would eventually win the lottery. This was a joke I learned a while back and used it with procrastinators.

Finally, they cursed God in church saying, "Why haven't we won yet?"

God finally replied in a deep voice, "You might have a chance at winning if you decide to actually go out and buy a ticket."

Then, a nurse who I had treated in the past came in to see me. I will call her Patty. She had a Bachelor's Degree in Nursing from a prestigious university and graduated at the top of her class. Most of all she was very caring and compassionate. She went that extra mile for people. If anyone deserved to be a nurse, she did. She was very sensitive, but perhaps too much so. She would modify her emotions with opioids and escalated her use. She became an opioid addict over time and hid it well. She told me a story where a premature infant from a drug addicted teenage mother died in her arms, after she cared so hard for it. She wept uncontrollably as she recalled the story. I sat in utter silence. I failed Patty however in the long run. She wrote prescriptions for herself, forged another providers signature and was caught. She lost her license and spent time in prison. She was self-medicating her emotional pain. I advocated for treatment but the legal system felt she had to pay her debt first. She did "dry out" in prison. After she was released she sought me out. I did visit her several times when in prison and comforted her as best I could. I told her that we should talk. I told her that I would try to see her the following week and come up with resources. She agreed and the next week we met at Tim Horton's for coffee. She told me I looked tired. She told me that I was burning out and to try to find peace, and put her hand on my cheek.

"You are a good man." She told me, "People need you." I failed to see all the signs however.

She was very down and tried suicide in prison but her attempt failed. She felt she let everyone down, including me. Her lips quivered as she mustered a smile for me.

I told her to let me put her in a hospital but she resisted, and said, "Honestly I'm not suicidal, please don't do that –all I need is good rehab now." Please help me was written all over her face. She came to me and I dropped the ball.

I gave her at least ten good referrals. She kissed me softly on the cheek, gave me a hug and thanked me. I told her to follow up with me next week and if I did not hear from her that I would call her. She agreed to do this, and left with a hesitant smile. The next week she was dead. The Grim Reaper put out his hand in some cold, dark city alley and she reached back to grasp it. As a result she was whisked away to a dark void. Her light and beauty gone from this world forever. She was found in a seedy side of town battered and bruised in this alley, possibly seeking drugs and apparently died of overdose---so I was told by her brother. She may have also been killed by someone but no one knew exactly. I went to her funeral and wept. I could not go back to my practice for a week. I miss her very much to this day, and can see her face the last day I met with her. The sadness overwhelmed me. I had always wondered what I could have done better. Slowly this profession was eating at me like a cancer I could not control. I started to think about getting out more and more. I was looking for an out. I was very disillusioned. One of my colleagues who is much older and with much more time invested in this profession saw the reality. He told me one day, "I do not see you aging out in this profession Tom." I quietly nodded in agreement, and then slowly walked away. He called out after me, "and that's too bad for this profession,"

The following month, I was slow to start but I had yet another "unusual" case. A woman came in with her puppy, a beautiful little beagle, very friendly little dog. It reminded me of my dog who was assassinated.

My secretary said to me, "Well, she's depressed and you might want to evaluate her for anti-depressant medication."

I said, "Ok, send her in."

Now, generally as a rule we really don't allow pets in the office, but I made an exception because this lady seemed so attached to this dog and it probably was good therapy for her depressive state.

I was playing with the pup and asking her questions like, "Well, Ma'am, how long now has this depression been going on?"

She replied, "Oh, since birth."

I said, "Since birth? Oh my Lord. That's an awfully long time to be depressed. What are the symptoms?" I prodded.

"Sad face, sad look, tired, probably tearful and irritable at times."

"What does your husband say? I stated.

"Well," she replied, "he doesn't seem to care or pay attention."

"Oh my, that's terrible," I replied in amazement. I'm thinking *how could her husband not care about her? What type of cruelty is this?*

"Well," I said, "we might want to consider an anti-depressant medication, perhaps a low dose and go from there.

She said, "That's what I've been thinking."

"Good," I replied. "We are both in agreement! I would also recommend counseling with me at least one time per week for now as well," I added.

She then stated, "Can I ask a question of you, Dr. Tom?"

I replied, "Of course,"

"How exactly do you conduct psychotherapy with a dog?" she said.

I replied, "Excuse me; I'm not sure I know what you mean."

"Well," she went on, "if you are willing to put Foo-Foo, her puppy, on an anti-depressant, how do you do counseling with her since she can't talk to you back, or maybe you're like Caesar, The Dog Whisperer, right?"

I sat stunned with a blank look on my face. *I'm thinking all along we're talking about the dog, not her.*

I said, "So let me understand this. You're fine; it's Foo-Foo who is depressed."

"Yes, I thought you knew this," she replied aghast that I didn't know this.

Caesar would be appropriate. Then I realized I knew a psychiatrist who has a dog and he is close to this dog and keeps it on his lap when he interviews patients. I'm told he had given his dog Prozac, an anti-depressant, and gives it brief therapy sessions. *Perfect,* I thought. I gently explained to her that I had the perfect doctor for Foo-Foo and he could evaluate her for anti-depressant medication as well.

She seemed pleased and said, "Thank you, Dr. Tom. You've been most kind and understanding."

I said, "You're welcome; anything for Foo-foo."

My secretary came back and said, "She left a happy camper."

I replied," Did you know it was not her, but the dog that was depressed?"

She laughed, "Yepper, she told me when she filled out the forms."

"I felt she was projecting her feelings on the puppy, or she was delusional."

"I referred her to Dr. Mayfair. Since he medicates his own dog, he would be the one to understand the issue better than I," was my reply.

"Good call," she said.

Then about a month later another woman came in and found out I was also an "animal shrink". She apparently knew this other patient who bragged about me curing her puppy. My desk phone suddenly came alive and it was my trusty and faithful receptionist.

She said, "Dr. Tom your next patient is here and she is a real pig."

I retorted back, "That's not nice to call our patients pigs and if she is that messy please tell her to use the trash receptacle in the waiting area."

Then my receptionist replied tersely, "No! You don't get it, she's a real pig, like oink, oink."

"Alright," I stated, "I'm coming out."

Before I could rise from my chair, the door slowly creaks open but no one is there. It is the spy I once treated or perhaps the invisible man is having marital issues. Then a grunting sound is heard. I look down and low and behold, it is indeed a pig. The swine runs past me and promptly jumps on my couch and looks at me sardonically.

"Please feel at home" I say to the pig like it can understand me.

While keeping a watchful eye on the potentially sociopathic pig, my receptionist calls me on the phone laughing aloud, stating "That's your next patient Dr. Tom."

I reply aghast, "That's a pig!"

To which she sarcastically replies, "Oh, you think?"

I can hear her hanging up laughing again. I'm thinking I hope the pig has good insurance.

As I turn to the pig, a tall, slim woman comes in before I can close the door.

She says, "I see you met Minerva, Dr. Tom."

"Minerva?" I questioned.

"Yes sir, she is my pig. I love her dearly, but she is depressed you see."

"Well," I reply, "I do not treat animal's really only homosapians sapiens-humans."

"We can pay in cash," she states, "whatever your hourly rate Doctor."

So I say immediately, "You're right she does indeed look depressed and probably could use counseling."

"Thank you, I knew as did Minerva that we could count on you." I am the pig whisperer.

As I motion for this lady to sit down I pull out my pad and pen to take notes.

"So, what brings you in Miss?" I question.

She replies, "My name is Sam short for Samantha, and Minerva's husband left her for another girl."

Suddenly I notice Minerva's ears perk up and she blurts out a huge grunt.

"What did she say Sam?" I ask.

"She wants help in dealing with her husband leaving her for another pig," Sam states

I suddenly look at Minerva, who then looks at Sam, who then looks at Minerva, and then they both look at me. We all stare at each other in silence. Finally, I think *what's happening now? Is the pig and Samantha in telepathic communication? Why are they looking at me?* Silence is deafening. *Am I really at home in bed dreaming?*

Finally, Sam speaks up and says, "She wants you to talk with her not me Dr."

I then reply, "Well I don't' speak pig or even pig Latin."

Another grunt erupts from the pig.

"What now?" I reply.

Sam states, "She is hurting because that pig left me...I mean Minerva for another woman...I mean pig."

Sam blurts out "They are both pigs my husband and the pig he left me for."

I say, "You mean Minerva-right?"

Silence.....

Then Sam blurts out again, "Yes of course I mean Minerva. Who did you think I meant?" I replied, "You're going to think I'm crazy but I kind of felt like we were talking about you."

Sam replies, "You're good Dr. Tom, You're good."

I reply, "Yeah! I'm a regular Sherlock Holmes."

She uses her pig as a metaphor and projects through Minerva, if indeed that is Minerva's real name. With the truth revealed, Minerva grunts and jumps off the couch walking past me, staring at me with a grimace.

"Both Minerva and I thank you," Sam stated.

The following session, Sam made it known that she and her pig, not her husband but, Minerva decided to file for a trial separation. I applauded her courage and Sam was pleased with her progress in therapy. Sam then suddenly placed sunglasses on her pet pig. I bit my tongue so as not to laugh.

I stated, "I did not know pigs wear sunglasses."

"Sometimes", Sam replied, "Minerva gets sensitive to light."

"I see" I said to Sam.

Then silence...which was suddenly broken by a loud sound, like a small explosion. Again, I know it's not me. I look at Minerva who looks at Sam who looks at me. Then Sam quietly points to Minerva, who again looks at Sam and grunts.

"So, what just happened?" I ask Sam.

"Well Minerva apologizes." Sam states, "She's had gas all morning."

I'm thinking *yeah-right, Minerva again.* Sam smiles coyly. Session ends and they both leave happier. Nevertheless, my receptionist used Fabreeze on my couch after Minerva left admonishing me not to take any more pigs on. That was the end of my animal therapy until a year later when a lady came in with her cat on a leash claiming it was possessed, but that was another story. I had to perform an exorcist on this cat at the end.

The strange things I had to deal with in thirty years that they did not teach in graduate school.

The following week, I fielded a call from my brother who is a physician in a hospital and was working a shift in the ER. He told me he had a strange "psych" case. The police had brought in a naked woman in handcuffs. She was running around a nearby park yelling strange words that were not defined, like made-up words, and the words were jumbled together. The police brought her in to be triaged through the emergency room and he was to do an evaluation. He went on to say she was calm, almost serene looking and she was very attractive. Caught up in her affect and good looks, he asked the policemen to remove the cuffs. The officers did not think this wise.

My brother stated, "Look guys, she is calm now, it's ok."

The police stated, "Doc, no disrespect, but we don't think this is a good idea. She can turn on a dime."

"Nonsense," my brother said, doubting their veracity. The cuffs were reluctantly removed by the police and they stood a little back, possibly knowing what might come next, and giving the doctor room. My brother gently asked a nurse to put a gown on her and this occurred without incident.

My brother told me, "You're not confined and no one is going to hurt you. Now, what's your name?"

At that, she hauled off and punched him and he went flying backwards over the gurney. The police and nurse grabbed her, gave her a shot of sedative and tethered her to the gurney. The nurse put an ice pack on my brother's face.

"So, brother, what did I do wrong? She seemed so normal."

"How many years have you been practicing medicine?" I asked.

I told him it sounds like she was schizophrenic and off her medication if she was ever on medication.

I asked hesitatingly, "Did the psychologist or staff psychiatrist evaluate her?"

He replied, "They sent her to the psych unit."

"This," I added, "should have been done in the first place."

"Never, never get too close to a patient you do not truly know who is brought in naked and in handcuffs – Duh! This is Psychology 101. How's your face?" I asked very concerned.

He reported in a humble and embarrassing manner, "My pride was hurt more than I was."

"Live and learn, Bro, live and learn," I stated. I wasn't sure he would survive if he was in my field, I thought. Perhaps, however, he would, with my help.

One week later, I encountered a homeless person. She did not have insurance;

like having insurance was a huge benefit anyway given how patients are treated by some insurance companies. Nevertheless, she was initially turned away and sent to a community mental health center. However, I informed my secretary that I could do some pro-bono work. She looked at me funny; sort of that look one gets when you're constipated. Nevertheless, I said, I could see her for a few sessions. When she came in, she was completely disheveled and I could swear her hair was a bird's nest. As a matter of fact, I could have sworn a sparrow flew out of it. It was a huge, frazzled mess; like someone electrocuted her and her hair went straight up. I thought, *ok, talk about a bad hair day*, I think she had a bad hair month. So, I made it my mission to help her. I said to Reba, I think that was her name, no obvious relation to Reba McIntire,

"We are going to get you some new clothes, hairdo and lunch in that order."

I took her to a Salvation Army Center where they had donations and picked some sizes up for her, then took her down to a beauty salon and shelled out about sixty bucks, but I think I paid seventy given the difficulty of the task. Next, I bought her sandwiches, soda pop, and we ate lunch. The next few sessions, I did my best to help her out and put her in touch with people who could help her. I never saw her again. She disappeared. I subsequently called several of the agencies, but they had not seen her either. It's like the wounded little bird that falls out of the nest; you patch it up and it departs, never to be seen or heard from again. I had on occasion seen other homeless people and again brought them sandwiches or blankets and one an umbrella to help her when it rained. Anyone would have done this, but for me, it was like I was giving back. Even my partner brought a blanket from home for a lady we both took to. But try as I might, I couldn't get her off the street. I only rarely see her these days. Living on the street must be incredibly hard. Just driving by the homeless is heartbreaking enough. There are so many potholes I keep hitting. You would think I would just drive down another street. Then one night it was Halloween and my secretary went home early to go to a party. She told me I had one more couple but they would be in costume because they too are going to a Halloween party. After she left I looked out the desk window to see Batman sitting there in full costume, in my waiting room. Wow, even Batman has issues, of course after all he is the dark knight, and lost his parents when he was young-right? I motioned him into the room.

I told him, "I thought this was couples therapy."

He told me his wife was parking the car and would be in soon. I asked him if it was Cat Woman.

He said, "How did you know?"

Shocked, I replied, "It was a guess."

On cue, this very pretty "Cat Woman" came in as well.

She was quiet so I opened up and said, "Cat got your tongue."

She gave me a dirty look. They took off their masks and they were indeed a handsome couple. I could not understand why they had problems. Or maybe I could. After all, Batman and Cat woman are arch rivals, right? I discerned that the problem was her mother. She was always in their "nine lives" and this caused him to have "cat scratch fever" when she was around. They did not laugh at that either. I told him to try and fly under the radar with her. He told me that was not funny either. I thought it was after all he was a bat.

I said, "It was not meant to be funny", well sort of. I mean do not make everything a contest and take yourself out of the triangle with your wife. I explained how the drama triangle worked to keep the pathology in the cycle. I also gave them both strategies to deal with the situation which caused the least amount of harm. After six sessions, they sent me a letter stating that her mother found a male friend and is moving in with him and apologized for not being able to be in their lives so much. They thanked me but I thanked the male friend. We take what we can get sometimes.

I had a great experience with a man I will call Jake. He was also homeless and living out of his dilapidated old van. It was flea ridden and he brought fleas into the office. My receptionist and I were itching for days and had to bring in an exterminator. He was very angry at women and my receptionist, because she was a woman. I let most of what he said roll off my back until he threatened her one day. I then laid down the law, and he bucked up because he had been thrown out of other offices. He used to call me up and rage at me then call again and apologize. I treated him kindly however, gave him money to get food and gas, and set him up with a lawyer friend of mine to get on disability. All my work was free for him as he had no insurance. Although I understood his anger, he had been violated by his mother and other women as a child. I was dedicated to helping him. After he received his disability he sent me back the money I gave him with a letter of thanks. He has an apartment now and is dating a woman, a real woman not a blow-up doll, and has his life back. His anger abated. This is what it is all about I felt. I did the happy dance in front of my secretary and she laughed so hard I thought she would bust a gut as my dad used to say. I suck as a dancer.

I had another fantastic experience with a "felon" who I was pleased to have helped. I asked him to write a book about his experiences and "Someday I will", he told me. He had given me permission to tell a small part of his extraordinary story. I will refer to him as Colton. Colton came to my practice based upon a referral from Family Services. Colton was a family man, great father to three children and loving husband. His wife had a few addictions however and fighting eventually erupted in the family. Colton was a God-fearing family man who was a professional chef, bartender and host in very fine restaurants which catered to the upper crust in life, including movie stars he had said. As his marriage unraveled so did he. He was eventually charged for domestic violence even though he never assaulted his spouse he told me. She called the police during one of their altercations and he was charged even though he did not touch her. He reportedly had a female judge very sensitive to the plight of women in society. He called her a biased feminist, but not to her face, naturally. He was sent to jail. He was let go from his job, and when he was able to finally get a divorce was ordered to pay child support. Without a job and many bills adding up he could not stay afloat. He was now using drugs to self-medicate his bouts of anger and mood swings which had increased over time. He ended up in abusive relationships with amazon type women who had also used drugs and whom physically assaulted him. He looked like yesterday's diapers.

A once God fearing family man, he had now degenerated into the depths of the underworld. He started to sell drugs to help support himself and pay his child support. He played cat and mouse with both the police and underworld criminal types. He was in and out of jail and a variety of mental health systems that all misdiagnosed him and put him on a host of medication that did not work. Every time he could not pay his support he was jailed, finally ending up in The Big House with hard time. He had to fight to live, sometimes fighting the biggest guys just to survive. They would fight over a twinkee. He had more than thirty charges for various offenses. They included: domestic violence; assault; nonsupport of dependents; probation violations; alcohol and drug use; and intoxicated motor vehicle use while under the influence.

One time he led a police officer on a dangerous and long chase, hid under a viaduct, when he thought the coast was clear came out. The officer was waiting for him patiently on the other side. He later came to respect that officer and the officer him. He owed some drug people money and they held his girlfriend hostage threatening to kill her and his mother and father and children.

"I went insane then… you do not threaten my family." he told me. He called these individuals up and threatened them. They met and he too produced a weapon. There was what he termed "A Mexican Standoff." He was prepared to kill them he later told me. He could give them the money back "and they went away", he stated. He realized how dangerous things had gotten, how insane he had become. He knew he needed help. He spent many years in prison and became hard. He called prison "The Gladiator Tank". He did two things well: Build his body up and fight to stay alive. Sometimes he fought huge guys over Twinkies, HO HO's or Cupcakes. You do not mess with a man's Ho Ho's he told me.

He once told me "There is no rehabilitation in prison, only survival."

He would have to fight the largest guy just to establish his place.

"If you are weak you die" he informed me. "You learn to be a gladiator, and the guards genuinely do not care. After all you are a felon. There is absolutely no rehabilitation, and no one truly cares."

After many years, he had become more enlightened, read The Bible again and grew spiritual. He quieted the anger inside, helped teach reading and writing to other inmates. He had become a model prisoner. Eventually he was released but lost his driver's license, could not find work because he was a felon, and went back to jail over and over for nonpayment of child support. He continually was given time by his favorite female judge "who violated the standards of law" he later stated, as he found out later. He spent much time in the law library researching law. He wrote his own petitions. He finally used the system against itself to win over his case with a new judge. The last one finally lost an election bid he told me. He came to me for help and told me that Family Services thought highly of me and wanted me to assess him. I finally gave him a correct diagnosis per Colton and coordinated his medication with a psychiatrist I trusted. His Bi Polar Moods and Panic Disorder had finally been stabilized. His racing thoughts, intensive anger, and euphoric episodes calmed down significantly. He is drug and alcohol free now and wants to become a Pastor and work with our penal system to serve inmates. He meditates daily and reads the Bible. He exercises daily for several hours, and for one who is in his mid-fifties, is in excellent shape physically. He is in the process of finding housing now, and will soon go to Seminary College to fulfill his dreams.

"Oh and I want a dog too." he stated.

"What kind?" I asked him once.

He stated assuredly, "Why a Beagle, of course."

"Is there any other kind?" I laughed.

We are now friends long after I had treated him and I still encourage him on his dreams, even though I can only do twenty-five pushups while he does two hundred. I am so out of shape. I encouraged him to write a book to inspire others. He agreed to do so.

My business, however, continued to expand. Counselors were calling me wanting to work in my place in a variety of specialties such as substance abuse, trauma abuse, marital counselors, etc. I tried almost everyone, and started to interview psychiatrists. One psychiatrist was extremely good-looking, young, with basically movie star looks, and, amazingly enough played in a rock band at nights. Go figure! He had an inordinate number of female patients or fans. I always wondered why. So, what if he had movie star looks and played in a rock band, and was a doctor-right? Then a man came in claiming that he had a visitor two weeks ago. He was tall and trim; the man, not the visitor. He went on to say that, the visitor was small, only four feet tall and grey in appearance. I said, "So he was a little person, right?"

He said, "Well, yeah, kind of."

I said to this man, "What do you mean kind of?"

"Well he was ugly and approached my bed."

"Was this at night?" I stated.

"Yes sir, Doctor," he replied.

"Go on," I said, thinking this strange and wondering how this little man got in.

Well," he said, "he commanded me to do something strange."

"Go on," I prodded.

"Well, Doctor, I'm almost embarrassed to say."

"Please, go on, go on," I said, very intrigued now.

"Well, sir, he wanted me to make love to my dog."

Stunned, I said, "What?"

"You heard right Doc - my dog," he said.

"Wait a minute…. this little guy, who is grey in appearance with an obvious skin disease, wants you to make love, with or without a condom, to your dog?"

"Yes sir," he stated.

"So did you?" I said.

"Of course, Doc, he told me to and more than once, I almost was compelled and had no will of my own."

I'm horrified. Oh, I'm thinking diagnoses here - schizophrenia, delusional disorder, zoophilia (bestiality), psychotic disorder of some type?

"Do you know this man?" I stated, now genuinely horrified, but concealing my feelings. "It wasn't a man, Doctor" he replied.

"What do you mean it wasn't a man?" I inquired.

He replied, "It was them."

"It was who?" I said.

"Them," again he stated.

"No, I mean who exactly are them?" I replied.

"Aliens," he said.

I replied, "Aliens, like from another planet - aliens!"

He said "Yep, you got it Doc."

"So let me get this straight," I stated, "this alien, who you don't really know or recognize, and he's not a family member, comes to you in the night and asks you to screw your dog and you do it, correct?"

"Yes sir," he replied without any hesitation.

"So, do you always do what aliens tell you to do?" I said in amazement.

"No sir, Doc. This is the first time," he said.

I replied, "The first time you encountered an alien telling you to screw your dog or the first time you screwed your dog without an alien telling you?"

"Both," he replied.

"Ok," I said, "Please stay right there in my office. Now don't go anywhere and don't go with any alien no matter what he says, ok?"

"Ok, Doc," he replied.

I closed the door to my office shaking my head, went up front to talk to my secretary and told her to call the police. We need to take this guy to the hospital's psychiatric ward for an evaluation immediately. When I got back to my office, the door was open. I cautiously walked in, but the man disappeared. He may have heard me talking to my secretary and took off, or he disobeyed my request and went off with his alien friend. Nevertheless, I felt sorry for the dog. I had my secretary cancel the police call to the hospital.

She said thoughtfully, "Maybe it wasn't really his dog. Maybe his wife is a dog. You ever think of that? And it's really a dream or nightmare and he feels alien toward his wife - right?"

"Thanks, Sigmund. I'll take it under advisement," I told her.

"I'd make a good psychologist, don't you think?" she said without turning to me.

I replied, "You took the words out of my mouth."

I was talking with my father that night and he stated he didn't know how I did what I did day in and day out.

He said, "I'm surprised you don't have a psychologist."

I said with a humorous tone, "Dad, you're my psychologist."

"I guess I have been all your life," he replied back laughing.

"And you're the best dad," I stated.

My dad has always been my rock. He knew this too. He told my brother once that he worried about me, because he knew he would not live forever. He knew I was the more sensitive one between my brother and I. He knew I would take this hard, and he was right.

The following day, I called in dead. I had a crushing migraine headache complete with aura and nausea. I suffer from intensive migraines. Everything was amplified 10 times in the house. I could hear the tick tock of the clock without hickory, dickory or dock. It sounded like a sledgehammer. The teakettle went off. It sounded like it was a train whistle. The cat roared like a lion. If I had a gun handy, I would have first dispatched the cat, then me - murder/suicide! Thank goodness, I have had some physicians in the practice who write me a script for Propranolol or shoot me full of Tordol. This helps the pain to a degree.

Obviously, I put my stress or other people's stress in my head. There is one patient of mine who has an uncanny ability to foresee migraines in me. She frightens me a lot.

I try not to see her, because when she comes in, she says with a sly smile, "Dr. Tom, today's your day."

"My day for what, Paula?" I say cautiously back.

"You know, a migraine. You'll be getting one later on Dr. Tom," she says.

So, does she plant a hypnotic suggestion? However several hours later, I do indeed get one. Either that, or Paula is clairvoyant. So I avoid Paula at all costs, but she still manages to find me and put the curse as my father says, "of the seven geese upon you." I'm very sensitive to migraine sufferers everywhere and Paula apparently.

I said to Paula, "Look at my secretary. Can you tell if she will have a migraine today?"

"Oh no, Dr. Tom," Paula replied, "she's doing her womanly thing. She'll be cramping later on." Sure enough, my secretary cramped up.

She said, "You know that one counselor at that other agency who doesn't like you. So you are saying how about we transfer Paula to him?" I reply as if I am reading her mind.

"Yes and we are good to go," she smiled wryly.

In the meantime, I had done some lecturing to schools about the bullying problems. I lectured at a nursing home explaining Alzheimer's disease and Psychological Conditions in the elderly. I educated physicians, explaining the psychological aspects of irritable bowel syndrome leaving them. I thought, "When constipated, trust only movement," a statement made by Dr. Alfred Adler.

In the weeks to follow, I treated a depressed clown who came in complete clown suit. He came from a children's party and they were really cruel to him. One child shot him with his own seltzer bottle while another, he told me, tried to shoot him in the butt with a BB gun. He cried uncontrollably. I also treated a woman who claimed she was a vampire complete with darkened lips and sharpened incisors. Interesting as this is, however, she came out in the daylight and didn't seem to burn up. My secretary feared her and said maybe we should keep a gun in the office with silver bullets. I told her that was for werewolves, not vampires; get her night creature's right. I told her to wear garlic and she would be ok. She did not take my advice, however, so I told her I could not be held responsible for what might happen to her. She didn't laugh. After that, there was a plethora of religious artifacts in her office, including candles and crosses.

On my few days off, my goal was to remain as sane as possible. I golfed, flew, fished, raked leaves, cleaned gutters, swept the porch, cleaned toilets, chased gophers, tried to catch a running duck - did anything to distract my mind. Since I live in a forest, literally, I could sit down on a tree stump and quietly watch the squirrels play or deer come up to a salt lick or blue jays fly from tree to tree and be one with nature. This was my hour, my therapy and it was generally very relaxing. One time I had a butterfly land on my shoulder. They say that was good luck, but I'm still waiting for my good luck. Then I saw a female praying mantis eating her mate after mating. I empathized with the guy.

The next day, I had yet again to fight the good fight with an insurance company. They

wanted me to sign a waiver form. They wanted me to change my diagnosis to fit theirs and if they were wrong, they wanted me to take the liability, especially if this individual was medicated and the medication caused harm. They told me how many sessions I could have, if I could do testing or not, and if I could refer for medication or not, dependent on whether their nurse felt it was appropriate. She would, however, consult with one of their psychologists or social workers. Don't you love it? I had done some therapy with a patient who worked claims and authorizations for one of these companies. She admitted they did not really care for patients and it was all about cost saving at the expense of the doctors, therapists and even patients. She did not have to tell us this. I figured this out. I was one hour late in authorizing testing for a patient and one company refused to pay anything on our authorization. They would not even backdate. We wrote it off. Basically, if things are not authorized on time, or if a diagnosis is not authorized by the insurance company it is not used. You and the patient are then screwed. I laughed when I received a check for a therapy session for .66 cents. Even a physician friend of mine had to go to an inferior generic medication, because it was cheaper than the one that worked for his patient. The sad part is the provider takes the heat generally, my patient who used to work for these companies, went on to say.

My physician friend said in a disbelieving howl, "They want to put us out of business, Tom. Sometimes, I can barely make my bills and I must figure out ways to cut costs without compromising my patients. It's maddening!" One of my professors had warned me not to go into private practice because the insurance companies completely control how much money you make, who you can see, what you can diagnose and if you can prescribe psychological testing or medication, all with the fact that they never even see your patient. It is disillusioning, but the absolute fact is they do not seem to care, per a patient I treated who once worked for an insurance company. Doctors cannot be doctors anymore. Everything in health care is big business this patient told me.

Perhaps it's not too late to become an ice road trucker. You work your own hours and the pay isn't too bad, I hear. I'm not as a rule, a super religious person, but one cold and lonely night I snuck into our Church. It was very dark and very quiet. I could hardly see the pews. I sat down in a pew and asked God why I couldn't help everyone who came to me, why I had to fight so hard with these health insurance companies to get the services I need, why people couldn't just try to be a little better toward each other, more loving. Feeling beaten and disheartened, I could have sworn I heard a soft voice say behind me or above me whisper, "Persevere, just persevere." As I looked behind me, a bit frightened, I could have sworn I saw a shadowy figure, but it disappeared as I turned around and glanced over. I was nervous and hairs on my neck stood up. I slowly walked to the shadow. But nothing was there. I was very alone. My emotions wrecked me then and there. I honestly wasn't delusional, psychotic or under the influence. I whispered into the universe, "Thank you." Then I quietly walked out of the church. I chalked it off to stress.

Suddenly, I was approached by a nosy neighbor in her night overcoat. The angry woman in her pajamas wanted to know who I was and why I was in her church. She had given me another startle. I took a deep breath and turned to face her.

"Just talking to God," I told her matter of factly, "Just talking to God."

She left saying she would call the police if I came back and would talk to the pastor about forgetting to lock the church at night. I told her I had a key given to me by the Pastor then quietly left. I never forgot that experience at the church and told no one, because I could see the headlines, "Dr. Tom, local psychologist locked in Psych Unit." Was God somehow there with me? Was I cracking up myself? Did my eyes play tricks on me or my ears? Was the stress of working 12-16 hours per day taking its toll? I didn't know, but I carried on the next day at work. I did want to persevere despite the odds and challenges. I enjoyed trying my best to help people. I was passionate in my purpose. I would continue to work hard, because if I could at least help one person, I would feel as if I made a difference in someone's life. I know this sounds cliché, but it is how I felt and still feel because. My father once told me, "We are only here for a visit so make your time count." He added that sometimes we have to fight the things that matter the most to get the results we want. "Life is never really easy, is it son?" he lectured. I replied, "people are never really easy either are they dad?" He replied back, "what is it Shakespeare said, but to thine own self be true." I think I got his message.

He was right! I always wondered about the voice I heard in the church late that night. Stress does a funny thing to a fellow.

The following week, I saw a woman who cried almost uncontrollably in my office. She was verbally abused by her husband who called her a whore.

I said to her with a clever look, "Are you one? Do you get paid for your sexual services?" I was "spitting in her soup" so to speak.

Indignantly and angrily she said, "Of course not! How could you say that, Doctor Tom?" I then said tersely, "Well, maybe then you're really a tree, right?"

"Tree?" she replied curiously. She was baffled as her face betrayed her confusion.

Then she laughed, stopped crying and started laughing and said, "That's silly. Of course, I'm not a tree and you're really a doctor, right?"

"I know what I am, but you don't know what you are. "I stated plainly.

"Of course, I do, but I'm not a tree," she replied.

"You're not a whore either," I said, "so why did you laugh when I called you a tree, yet cried when you're called a whore. We both know they are both silly and you are neither, right?" She sat dumbfounded and stared at me in silence, thinking deeply about what had just transpired.

Suddenly the silence was broken by Laughter as she spoke, "Dr. Tom, you're alright. I get it. So why am I so upset?" "Exactly," I said.

She looked at me and said, "You're good!"

"I'll see you next week again Doctor. Thanks!"

I'm thinking, *another satisfied customer, guaranteed success or your neurosis back.*

Three weeks later, I went into a store to get some duct tape. Did you know you can do just about anything with duct tape, like take off warts? Some research, which is mixed, has demonstrated that putting a small piece of duct tape on a Wart over several weeks could remove it. Of course, there may be easier ways to remove warts, however, I would still check with your physician. Never the less, as I exited the store, a little boy apparently followed me out. He probably left the side of his parents and walked out behind me. Something caught my eye and I looked behind me. As I started to enter the street to cross it, this three or four-year-old did the same. A car was coming and I scooped him up and put him back on the curb, as the car passed us both. As soon as I did this, his mother came out, gave me a dirty look, told me to do something sexual to myself and grabbed her child and went back into the store. Again, I thought of what Ben once told me, *"No good deed goes unpunished."* Another lady came up to me and said she had seen what I did and replied, "You saved her kid. Why wasn't she watching him?" "I don't know," I replied back, "but if I don't scram now, I will probably be arrested for attempted child abduction ma'am. By the way, thanks for your support." As I left, I kept looking behind me thinking I'm going to be doing group therapy in Attica, and have a new "girlfriend" called Bubba.

I was working with a firefighter who had anger management issues. He was obsessive, compulsive and everything "had" to be exactly his way. No doubt, he had a smattering of a personality problem as well and even his wife couldn't take it anymore and threatened divorce. Once I ruled out Bipolar Disorder and Borderline Personality Disorder, I had gotten him on some anti-depressants and blood pressure medication, many blood pressure meds. We did a lot of changing of his thinking and relaxation therapy strategies. This guy was wired for sound. I told him the story of the Samurai and the Dragon, a Zen Parable. This is a story Ben gave me years ago, and I kept it. It did not have an author on it for me to give credit. I searched but to no avail. I used it with this client however and it helped him. The story goes like this.

"Now it didn't make book sense, but I found myself liking this tired old dragon with his scarlet scales and great five-clawed feet. I felt like a prince as I rode on the back of the dragon. From this position, high on his humped back, I noticed that the

Dragon's body was covered with old wounds. Whenever the dragon breathed forth fire to light the path in front of us, I noticed that the wounds glowed golden-red in the dark. I also noticed dragon limped now and then, but as it was the end of the day, I thought that he must just be tired. The old wounds did, however, arouse my curiosity, and when I asked about them, the dragon replied "Oh, my friend, I have been slain a thousand times, but I have always arisen again. These old wounds are a source of my power and my insight and even wisdom:' as I said, our greatest and worst enemies are not the monsters who roam the forest or even wicked witches or evil wizards. No, it is our scars, our wounds and old injuries that we must fear. As we Journey through life, we all have been injured; hurt by parents, brothers or sisters, schoolmates, strangers, lovers, teachers ... the possible list of the guilty is long. Each wound has the power to talk to us, you know. They speak, however, with crooked voices because of the scars. But allow me to tell you a story that will make my point even clearer. I was so caught up in the words of my dragon friend that I forgot my own weakness.

Once upon a time, began the dragon, a great Samurai warrior, very fierce indeed, who yielded two great swords, which hung from his belt, approached a monk and said, "Tell me, holy monk, about heaven and hell? The orange and brown robed monk slowly looked up at the warrior from where he sat and replied in a quiet voice, I cannot tell you about heaven and hell, because you are indeed much too stupid. Suddenly, without thought, the Samurai warrior was filled with rage. He clenched his teeth and his fists and gave a fierce shout as he reached for a sword. The monk then continued. Besides that, you are extremely ugly, he added. The Samurai's eyes flamed wide and his heart pounded incensed with 1mbridled rage and he raised the sword over the monk's head. "Now that," the monk said, "is hell." Struck, as if hit by a lightning bolt, the power of the monk's words hit home. The wisdom was so powerful indeed that the Samurai suddenly dropped his sword and fell to his knees, and bowed his head. And that, the monk said, is heaven.

You see, continued the dragon, the words spoken by the monk touched old wounds, perhaps wounds that were made when the warrior was a child and was made fun of and called stupid, dumb, or even ugly. It was his wounds, which that caused "hell" to capture him. All of us have wounds, old ones and new ones, and whenever the monster appears, when hell breaks loose, we know that our old wounds are talking and, of course, guiding us. It is those wounds, which must be confronted, not us poor innocent dragons. I said, your wounds glow with great beauty and you said, however, they are a source of your power and magic. How can wounds become a source of power?

First, replied the dragon, you must not give in the voice of your scars, the voice of the times you trusted and were betrayed, loved and were rejected, did your best and were laughed at. Do not give weight to the scars left because you were slighted or were made to feel less than others. Instead, when those voices call to you to react with envious or jealous feelings, do exactly the opposite. When they say run anyway, you must stay. When they whisper, distance yourself, then come all the closer. You must transform their power, not destroy it! That, my friend, is really being involved in a quest. All quests begin with some question. Great quests begin with great questions. Why am I not happy? Why am I not a Saint? How do I find happiness? That is exactly what you are questing after – happiness. And happiness, health, holiness, and all the rest come only when we have made our inquiries into glorious words.

The old Chinese dragon with the words that glowed so beautifully in the dark was indeed very wise. I saw how my behavior, which had so often hurt myself and others, had flowed from the fact that I had listened to the voices of some old wound. I realized what the dragon was saying to me. Yes, I must learn to listen to my pain as well as my pleasures. And I need to distinguish between the different voices I hear within myself, the voices of old wounds and the small quiet voice that comes from somewhere deep inside. It is this quiet voice that calls me to sacrifice, to generosity and to kindness, but it frequently has been outshouted by the angry voices of my old wounds. I have to begin a friendship with myself, with all myself. Perhaps the goodness that I have been seeking on my quest is really all inside me.

After I had processed this story with the angry firefighter, he started to quiet the flame that burned inside of him and started to heal his wounds. He, too, began his quest for self-discovery coming to peace not only with others, but especially with himself.

I guess the old story about teaching a man to fish is true. If you give a man a fish, you feed him for a day, but if you teach a man to fish, he feeds himself for a lifetime. Hopefully I taught him something for a lifetime.

It was around Christmas time now, and as I was driving to work, I heard a story over the radio. Santa Claus at a department store called 911 because one of the elves threatened the mall by claiming he was carrying a bomb. I'm thinking *even the North Pole isn't safe, either that or Santa Claus is a micromanager and has stressed out elves.* Maybe Santa pays low wages and cuts back on holiday pay like time off for Christmas and such. Nevertheless, the elf was apparently arrested and probably will be seeing a shrink for a psychological evaluation. However, this happened in another state, thank goodness and it would not involve me. Christmas seems to be the time when I see the most depression, alcoholism and/or suicidal thinking in people. Perhaps it's the lights, the thoughts of peace and joy and caroling in the streets that brings it out. Sort of like the full moon is to be a werewolf. Business goes up – sadly. It is a time when I would rather it be down. It is the time I do my best to get the homeless to a shelter, put a few extra pennies in the Salvation Army Kettle guarded by the Santa Claus who turned in his elf. I'm a little warier of elves now, and I wonder what lurks behind the wry smile of the Easter Bunny. Me, personally it's clowns – yes clowns. I've always had a clown-a-phobia. So how did this come about? When I was 6 years old I fell madly in love with the little 6-year-old girl down the street. Every time I saw her, I went into a sort of catatonic state with glazed eyes. I think her name was Susan, but I can't be sure now. We played together all the time and then something happened which drastically changed that relationship. She invited me to "The Bozo the Circus Show." This was back in the 1960's and the wait for tickets was at least 8 years. Her mother ordered those before she was born. She was so kind and thoughtful for inviting me. I was so excited! I had never been to a real live circus. I wanted to see The Great Bozo.

When I arrived with her mother and Susan in tow, we sat on bleacher type seats. At first the cameras, lights and stage performers were indeed wondrous and then …BOZO appeared. He came on suddenly as if out of the shadows; he came from behind a curtain. I remember his suit was very bright orange and his nose extremely red against his white make-up. I was suddenly tense, perspiration started to appear on my brow and forehead. My autonomic "nervous systems' "fight a flight" started in. The adrenal glands were pumping adrenal in an already overtaxed system. My breathing became labored and panic set in immediately. Suddenly, as if Bozo sensed there was a child in the audience who knew of "the power of clowns," he turned slowly and looked straight at me –like he had the force or something. I stiffened, gasped, and thought of Marlon Brando's words from Apocalypse Now – "The Horror, oh the Horror." He started immediately for me, reached out and I quickly jumped screaming from under my seat to the legs of my "girlfriend's" mother.

I was traumatized yelling out loud repeatedly, "Please, don't let Bozo eat me! Please don't let him get me!"

Now remember, I was 6 years old, and when we think about it, clowns have been mysterious and even deadly. Examples include: Killer clowns from Outer Space, Stephen King's "IT," and John Wayne Gacey's Clown. Even famed clown Emmett Kelly appeared very depressed. The technical, clinical word for fear of clowns is "Coulrophobia." This incident created this disorder in me – I was Coulorphobic. After this incident, Susan did not seem to want to play with me anymore. I can't say I could blame her, and she found a new boyfriend. I really suck with girls. Again, I was heartbroken by a girl – alone again naturally. Years later, I refused to attend circuses for that reason. I also noted that this fear of clowns transferred to other types of characters: Mickey and Minnie Mouse, Chip and Dale, the Chipmunks, and any other characters of a cartoon like variety. Then, once at a Disney World I was surprised and bushwhacked by Minnie Mouse who approached me on my blind side - as they so often do – and hugged me from behind. I suddenly turned in horror as a big mouse like face, which appeared with a frozen smile, gazed at me – giggling. She then left as suddenly as she appeared, leaving me with the stench of urine in my underwear and trembling with intensive fear. I've always wondered if Mickey knew what Minnie was doing to people on the side - yes traumatizing them! I also saw a small child about two or three run back to its' mother after an encounter with "Goofy." They don't call him "Goofy" for nothing you know. Have you ever thought of the mental health conditions of these characters, by the way? This is probably another book. To name a few, they have names like: Goofy, Daffy, Bugs and Dopey. This proves my point. We have some characters that apparently are not mentally well balanced, hence the traumatizing effect. To this day, I have challenged my fear of clowns and other cartoon characters by coming closer to them, but keeping a very wary eye. I have desensitized myself to them to some degree. Am I completely cured? Am I even normal? No. But, I am better. Santa does not create fear in me; however, I am cautious, especially of his elves ever since the department store incident. These creatures are easily identifiable, especially at the end of the year. They typically wear green suits, appear happy, although this might be beguiling, and dance around with jingle bells on their elf cap. One time I saw one with a tin flask kept under his elf suit. He shared this with his Santa who periodically looked around before taking a swig. I'm sure it was, however, only hot cocoa. They both did appear happier in mood. It must be good cocoa. I have never formally treated elves, Santa, clowns, or any of the seven dwarfs. Overall, challenging myself instead of avoiding things like clowns has helped me with other generalized fears. I've since read books like "Face the Fear and Do it Anyway" and passed that on to my patients who have benefited greatly.

I have a wonderful friend, a neuropsychologist who I have called Dr. Mark. I also call him "Indy," short for Indiana Jones. Dr. Mark is truly the real Indiana Jones. He has seen white sharks up close in South Africa with the Director of a famous Zoo. He has wrestled anacondas, searched for the Yeti in the Himalayas, been to the Amazon, smoked something with pygmies, tossed around a shrunken head, been held hostage by tribesmen, etc. … He had written books about his adventures, one in which I read with zeal on cryptozoology. He is an amazing man, friend and colleague who taught me much about psychology, neuropsychology, business and life. I will forever be indebted to people like him and Ben for their kindness, generosity and willingness to share their knowledge.

As Dr. M stated to me one time, "Life is an interesting adventure if you have the courage to go on the trip."

Every time I see him, I almost can hear the theme music for the Indiana Jones films playing in the background. He is truly a wonderful, magic and compassionate man, and these types seem rarer these days.

MANAGED CARE OR MANGLED CARE?

CHAPTER EIGHT

One of my patients worked for a health care insurance company, and I say worked for, past tense. To put it in her terms, "I left because I realized they did not always care about people, only their bottom line." As I stated earlier, almost on a daily or weekly basis, I must do battle with the giant "managed care." Sometimes I win, sometimes it wins. If I win, the patient wins. If I lose the patient may ultimately lose. Now, this is not to say that some of these organizations do not try to help their patients (my patients) or the doctors or therapists treating them. Some do. Most seem do not. I've been outright lied to as have my patients, disregarded, encouraged to use "diagnoses that will be paid for," sessions shortened, certain medications recommended only, etc. etc. etc. ...! Basically, as one of my colleagues has stated, "Our practices are not our own."

Studying the research on "managed care" indicates it is a rather complex system. However, to say that we need a reformed health care system is an understatement. Many who truly need it don't get it. If they get it, they either don't get enough of it or do not get any quality treatment and treatment at times is time limited. These companies say that they work for optimal care but the reality is quite different. Try to be a provider and then see what you can do or not do. My patients are very frustrated at the rising premiums and cannot find providers who are willing to take the lower rates. They go from provider to provider, or are delayed in getting care at all. If you have money, you can get more adequate care. If you don't, you take a number like everyone else and hope for the best. Doctors like me, physicians and therapists must work within the system and basically think outside the box presented to us to affect quality care as best we can. Some practitioners say if you can't beat them, join them. Jump the fence to either work for them, or do the best they can to work within the confines of the system, while others become lawyers. Since I'm still in debt on my doctorate degree, law school is not an option. Besides,

I'm not sure the legal profession would want me. It seems almost as if no one cares anymore about people or their plight or making the world a better, safer place for our children or children's children. I know this sounds cliché, but I feel there is some truth here. My mother states that Satan has taken over the world these days. I'm thinking it's more like it's people who have been greedy, misappropriated funding, too much economic borrowing, charging, feuding, etc. etc. etc., but who am I but a mere taxpayer with a clown phobia. Perhaps there are too many clowns in government, hence why so many people appear to be phobic about politicians who they think of as clowns. Again, like managed care, some do well I'd like to think, while others have underlying agendas. Nevertheless, I hope we can come up with a viable solution for the health care system. As I stated, it is complex, I have no definite solution, and I'm not politically savvy. I just don't want to look at a mirror, see a duck's reflection in it, and shoot the mirror instead of the duck. I don't want to be distracted by the fact that people in this country require viable health care that cares about their genuine well-being. The unspeakable issues with the veterans I treat and what they think of the V.A. and our government, especially the Vietnam vets. I'm sure I'll have my critics. But they'll have to stand where I am before they afford any criticism. There are other countless doctors who are frustrated and can't get the adequate care or funding they need to help their patients. Some cannot stay in practice, given the high cost of liability and practice costs. One of my close friends stated that her granddaughter, who is nine years old, needed a heart valve. Of course, the insurance company denied this even on appeal. They came up with some reason why they could not approve the funding.

My friend said, "Do we just let my little baby die?"

Her mother was furious and decided to go the media, after an intensive media blitz magically the insurance company turned their decision around and approved the procedure.

"Why?" the mother asked.

She stated, "It seems like the middle and lower classes are always the ones to suffer."

In one case, a managed care organization specifically requested a few of my notes to process a claim. I refused and they prohibited my claim from going through. Subsequently, they asked again citing the fact that they were entitled to these notes. They were per contract but I was suspicious and gave them a summary instead with the understanding that they not in any way share this with my patient because of the possibility of potential harm or misinterpretation. They verbally agreed. (I should have had this in writing.) Consequently, of course, they genuinely lied, gave copies of my notes and summaries to the patient without explanation. Subsequently, my patient did not fully understand clinical terms or the rationale for my decisions without me being there to explain. Prior to this, she and I worked very well together and she was improving. She was angry I wrote about her husband. She said that the whole hour was used for "relational issues" which she agreed it was, but that managed care was not paying for "marital issues," only individual problems, even though she talked for fifty minutes about her husband. She wanted me to perpetuate a fraud so I would get paid and she would not have to pay out-of-pocket for the session. I told her that her relational issues were part in parcel of her personal problems and she indeed used that time to talk about how that impacted her personally. The insurance company refused to pay (understandable if she was fraudulent) and she fired me as her doctor (psychologist) threatening to sue both me and the insurance company. I lost a patient who I was making strides with. The insurance company found a way to get out of paying me for my services, instead of working it out. They breached my confidentiality (summaries) to the patient after I specifically asked them not to given the consequences. I could have worked this out if they would have discussed this with me. So, ask me if I trust them when their motive is to curtail costs at the expense of doctor-patient relationships and therapeutic progress. You just can't win. Other "clinicians" must learn how to write notes to specifically comply with managed care objectives/standards to survive at the expense of being fraudulent to survive. Some of these insurance companies want us to change our diagnoses to theirs to get paid, even though we as the therapists and doctors are sitting with the patient. How is that ethical? Even the State Psychology Board will not fight these companies, they are too powerful. The world has different perceptions than me. It seems at times no one cares and the only thing that matters is cost. I'm sure many of my colleagues have similar tales. Then they report you to your State Board for being unethical, and the Boards appear to support them. Then you hire a lawyer and hope for the best, which may be the worst, especially if your lawyer does not challenge things. Once you have a restriction on your license or even a letter of reprimand, it is time for a new career. No one takes a chance on you no matter how good you really are or if the State Board made a grievous error. People believe that these Boards are very ethical, because they put trust in these systems to do the right thing, but they do not at times and can be self-serving. Some others are while others are not. The issue always comes down to people, and how fair and just they are. A judge once told a colleague that both lawyers and judges bend the law to fit what they perceive the situation calls for.

I thought things were to be objective, again the human factor. Are we not however to do the very best we can and be fair and just, is not this what America stands for? Did we lose sight of what are forefathers fought for? I wonder what they would say if they could look at our nation now. America is a truly great country but it needs tweaking. I want to believe that when it comes down to it people would want to do the right thing, but I have all too often seen the opposite sadly. I am too idealistic for my own good I think.

State Boards are given a lot of latitude and discretionary power. They have much immunity around them, given to them by the legal system in their infinite wisdom. The Supreme Court case Chevron USA Inc. vs. Natural Resources (1984) illustrates my point of abuse of power. This case in a nutshell, set forth per The Supreme Court, a legal test to determine whether to grant deference to a governmental agency's interpretation of a statute which it administers. Basically, this gave a Visa card to state administrative agencies to do whatever they want. It is like they have a protective bubble around them like the aliens in The War of the Worlds, movie. Absolute power corrupts absolutely. We must take in the human factor (subjectivity not objectivity). Lawyers and the legal system have stretched this interpretation out to go beyond what the Supreme Court meant in their Holding.

I'm sure the higher court did not say, "You are free to abuse the power and interpret this any way you desire."

Some Boards have ethical integrity others do not and literally abuse their power. This is a fact some will not admit of course. Every Board is defined by a culture like any organization, if they (the culture) are truly earnest and just they can be fair and restorative to members, if they are not their effects can be devastating. A Board is comprised of people who have different personalities or pathologies. Fair or not, they make decisions. You only get a shot at justice, not necessarily justice. This is very frightening. Per three lawyers I talked to about State Boards, they all agreed that in better than 60-70 percent of cases they had brought to higher courts concerning state board issues, the courts side with the Boards. In those other cases the decisions are negligible. This was their opinion.

Another illustration would be to read the book, *In Harm's Way* by Doug Stanton. The Naval Board (Military Board) essentially scapegoated a fine naval officer who dedicated his life to the service. Even his crew backed him up and fought for justice. Charles B. McVay III, was court-martialed for his dereliction of duty in the sinking of The Indianapolis in World War Two. The court even brought in Commander Mochitsura Hashimoto, the Japanese submarine commander who sunk The Indianapolis, adding insult to injury. However, Hashimoto stated that even though McVay did not set up a zig zag course he still would have sunk the ship. Captain McVay was destroyed emotionally and later committed suicide. Who sits with that? Years later and with congressional members and surviving crew members McVay was exonerated, much too late.

If a psychologist ever comes before one he or she needs very aggressive and competent legal representation. This is not easy to find I found out. I am not sure what they teach law students today but every lawyer I have encountered does not seem to put the energy into fighting for justice anymore. I am frustrated with this. State Boards are supposed to safeguard the public welfare which is necessary, it is when they act in a self-serving or biased manner that harm comes, and it is difficult to undo this harm. I have seen cases like this where truly gifted psychologists have gone to ruin based upon overzealous State Boards, who as one attorney told me "collect scalps" as their goals. This has a domino effect on not only that psychologist but the clients he/she serve. I will talk more about my State Board later. I have envisioned myself in a western gunfight, like as in the film Shane with Alan Ladd, who had a gunfight with Jack Palance as Wilson, an evil gunfighter, when I think of dealing with State Boards. Nevertheless, let us return to the managed care industry.

Per a survey, I read, concerning the effects of managed care, (I do not know the validity of this survey or who conducted it) 9 out of 10 doctors in a nationwide survey said they had patients who have been denied care by health insurers. They feared for the effect on a patient's health, physical and mental. Furthermore, practitioners tend to exaggerate the severity of illness according to this survey, just to get an insurer's approval to provide any kind of care. The study found that denials of coverage for mental health services have the most profound effect on patients' health, with nearly two thirds of the doctors surveyed saying that treatment denial in the mental health area caused a "somewhat serious 'or' very serious" consequence, up to and including suicide. The study, which I do not care to mention for obvious reasons; and I honestly cannot recall the title or cite, was based upon a national survey of 1,821 doctors and nurses chosen at random.

Furthermore, the survey goes on to say that disagreements over prescription drugs is the most common complaint, with 61 percent of doctors saying at least once a month, they must argue with an HMO over a prescription. Most fights occur when a physician feels a patient benefits from a name brand drug versus a generic brand. The stakes are higher; however, when a doctor and the HMO disagree over authorizing a diagnostic procedure like an MRI or psychological testing. 42% of the doctors surveyed in this study said they argue with HMOs over diagnostics at least once a month.

Within the managed care industry, current incentives generally do not encourage an emphasis on quality of care, despite what they say. Consolidation of the managed care industry has created great pressure for competition based almost exclusively on price.

Managed behavioral health care plans do differ considerably in their access and other aspects in terms of quality in mental health care. Current practices, however, often provide little incentive to improve quality and are generally based more on cost effectiveness. More outcome assessments and studies need to be promoted to discern evidentiary effects on people's health given cost-cutting measures. The bottom line is to genuinely help people improve their lives.

THE APOCALYPSE
CHAPTER NINE

Now back to our original story line. This is where it gets interesting. On or about sometime in 2010, I received a letter from My State Board. They told me they were opening an investigation on me for Fraud. A seventeen-year old's mother, who I had a supervisee do a "preliminary or initial" intake, filed the complaint. Again, what have I done to deserve this? Thus, the only attorney I knew was the one who set up my business. He assured me that even though he had no experience with state boards, he would consult with others who had. I was initially skeptical but decided to put my faith in my attorney----big mistake. You are supposed to trust you lawyer –right?

This woman brought her son because he went to a party and had one sip of a beer and she felt he may be alcoholic. She wanted him psychologically tested and evaluated for alcohol. She had a very conflicted relationship with him. After my supervisee evaluated him per my directions and under my supervision, she herself felt the mother to be very demanding and abrasive. I had a secretary who made a series of errors which I caught later. She told this woman that we took her insurance, when in fact we were out of network. However, it truly was the client's responsibility to determine if we took her insurance or not. This means she could still have the assessment but that she would have to pay out of pocket. Thus, I was willing to bring the price of the assessment way down. All the consent forms were given her, but she refused to sign them, unbeknownst to me. My new secretary did not follow up on this and did not write "refused to sign" on the form, as she was asked to do in situations where the patient refused to sign. The woman insisted that the evaluation proceed as she felt we were very good and came highly recommended. I made a subsequent error by proceeding with the intake because I wanted to help this woman and her son. As well I inadvertently checked marked the wrong box stating my supervisee was a "training" supervisee vs. a "work" supervisee. My supervisee did tell the woman and her son that she was a supervisee and that I would be supervising her closely on the case, which I did. I told the Board that my supervisee was well qualified because she came out of a "clinical" B.A. program. The Board admitted they never saw anything like this before and she (my supervisee) set a new precedent. As a matter of fact, my supervisee was only doing "initial" intakes; other B.A. level supervisee's do testing and more extensive intakes. The Board denied this. I told them that they were not in the trenches so to speak but this is indeed happening. I think administering psychological testing is more critical that doing an information gathering initial intake.

Nevertheless, both the son and his mother gave verbal consent, and they liked my supervisee. I should have written this down but did not catch this until later on. Limits of confidentiality were explained and my supervisee proceeded with the consent of both parties. The son told my supervisee that he had a very difficult relationship with his mother and she was always angry at either him or his father. He did not want his mother to get the intake, however because he was not yet 18 years old she had a right to see it. My supervisee wrote conservatively however, to protect possible abuse by mother to son. Unfortunately, this State does not care about this, as the parent has a definite right to information on clients who are deemed "minors" under the law. I consulted a lawyer on this and he told me a minor is not protected under this State's law, in other states it's different. This was scary news. The mother insisted she wanted all the testing information as well.

When I went before the State Board, I was very honest and told them of all the minor errors I had done. However, there was absolutely no harm done to anyone. They knew this. I told them that the mother could have halted the process at any time but insisted we proceed, and that was the honest to God truth. I however, did not get this in writing. The mother was very pleased with the intake my supervisee had done and was looking forward to the testing. It was explained to her that I would be doing a more formal intake or clinical interview as well. Again, she was pleased with our results.

During my supervision sessions with my supervisee it was determined indeed that this adolescent took only one drink at a party. This per the Diagnostic and Statistical Manuel of Mental Disorders did not constitute a diagnosis of alcohol Dependence or even Abuse. He was not intoxicated, or suffered any consequences thus, despite the Executive Director insisting that alcohol abuse should have been diagnosed. I told him that I was an expert in this area and being ethical meant that I could not diagnose him with what he did not warrant. He did not take this well, and registered some anger. He lost his objectivity. We also argued over the fact that my supervisee wrote a "tentative" diagnosis in her hand writing down. I told this Executive Director, who had a very stern face, that this was not a child, but an adolescent who had rights.

He got very angry and stated emphatically that, "This is a child!"

I told him that the legal system determines who is a child because in some cases some 15-year-old "children" are sometimes tried as adults. I tried to explain to him then why do we in psychology (and with the State Board Rules) have separate categories for children and adolescents, if there is a demarcation line? He kept insisting, "This is a child according to the law." He was also so very condescending to me. My attorney whispered for me to back off as I would lose on almost every point I made. So, I'm thinking then why not just take me out and hang me, what is the point of this?

Getting back to my story, my supervisee who is very calm and rational managed to calm this mother down, and she was pleased. She told her not to worry about any payment. She calmed down. Unfortunately, my secretary, who I later discovered was a closet alcoholic, attacked this woman every time she called telling her that she must pay regardless if we take her insurance or not. I knew nothing of this. An already angry mother was fueled up even more now. Later, I was told my secretary even reached through the glass to get her. I need this right?

One counselor told me that the mother shouted out expletives and this counselor told her she was, "Crazy and completely irrational."

This may be the case but how professional are we when the secretary, in a mental health facility, reaches out to grab her, and a counselor tells her she is crazy.

So as if things were not bad enough, they went from bad to hideous, and my biller got into the act. She sent this client a bill for the service again without my knowledge. So, let's pour gasoline on the already raging fire. This is when she reported me to the Board. The mother told them that she did not want a trainee to do the intake because she felt she was not qualified. She openly lied to the State Board, the reality was she wanted the intake for free, and was angry because she did not get this. My supervisee was aghast at what this mother did, because she knew what the mother actually told her.

"She boldfaced lied to the board, because she liked what we did and they both liked me," she said angrily. "She just wanted things for free," she went on to point out.

I told her sarcastically, "You think?"

I fired my secretary that day. In the end, the lady got her evaluation for free as she desired, it was a very good evaluation and she was referred on to another professional that I trusted would help her, and he did.

At this point I must backtrack in time a bit in this story.

Prior to the secretary that created problems with the mother and son who reported me, I had a different secretary. If you think the one I described earlier was bad, this one was the incarnate of evil. She called almost daily for a job with me.

She heard, "I was kindly and good."

She was also out of a job and needed money bad. I felt sorry for her. My wife, who was my part-time office manager, liked her and she hired her on---another mistake. I called in her last reference at a doctor's office, but was unable to talk with the doctor. I did talk with the staff who told me that all they could say was that they would not hire her again because she was manipulative and deceitful. I talked this over with my wife, and then she had her doubts. She told me to give her a chance but watch her. I also hired a trauma therapist who created additional trauma for me. She became "friends" with this new secretary. This was the beginning of my downfall after almost thirty years in this profession unscathed. A colleague of mine who is a psychiatric nurse practitioner, worked with the trauma therapist.

He told me, "I can't believe you hired her, she hates men."

Well she too was out of work and she came across as very professional at the interview. He then stated, "Good luck, but you're a dead man walking Tom."

As if that is not bad enough, Dr. Mark, my buddy the neuropsychologist came in.

He says, "Have you lost all your marbles?"

I replied, "What are you talking about?"

He comes back with, "Fire your secretary immediately."

"Why would I do that, I just hired her three weeks ago," I replied.

To which he says, "She is a Borderline Personality if I ever saw one—don't trust her at all, get rid of her now before it's too late."

I thought he had spent too much time in the upper regions of mountains or whatever he smoked with pygmies went to his head. It turns out however he was as right as rain. I again paid for my naiveté, and my strong desire to help others.

The State Board dismissed the Fraud case against me. The Executive Director was concerned about the supervision of a Bachelor's degree candidate, who despite her "clinical" training was still an undergraduate and not in a graduate program. However, under "umbrella" supervision and under "aide" category I was authorized to supervise her. Her degree was more in line with clinical counseling even though she was under a degree program overseen by the Psychology department. My inept lawyer failed to tell the Board that they cannot decide what rule applies and what rule doesn't, when there is a specific rule that does indeed apply. As well under umbrella supervision and under an aide category I could indeed supervise her. The lead investigator found no problem and felt I would be able to continue to supervise my supervisee. I later found out that after my case she resigned from the Board. Again, my lawyer remained silent time and time again not challenging the rule bending by this Board. For three hours, I was under hot interrogation. I felt criminalized. The Executive Director told me that he felt this evaluation that the supervisee did was over her head. I told him I did not agree, but for the sake of argument let's assume you are right. She is still under my supervision and this is all about teaching, I am totally responsible for this case and I have not finished it yet. This mother was completely satisfied with everything except she did not want to pay, that is why she called you and lied.

The Director said "You allowed your supervisee to diagnose because she wrote the diagnosis in her own handwriting."

I told him this was an "initial" intake and used for training purposes not the final one which I would conduct. He told me if it is in writing it is the truth. I said that is not necessarily the truth or logical and later I found out he reversed his own statement on this when we talked about what people stated to him did not comport with what they wrote. Then he took what they told him to be true not what they wrote. My lawyer stated that the Board is out of control, yet he did not challenge them or take them to court fearing I would lose. I stated to him lets be like a good detective and just follow the evidence, and he said no. I never understood this.

Nothing was taped and the only notes that were taken were by the Executive Director. Again, I admitted to Form violations, and the Executive Director suggested no formal hearing was necessary. They would negotiate a minor consequence, perhaps taking a workshop on forms and supervision. I was good with that. Despite my lawyer saying nothing and being subjected to three hours of intensive questioning I was let go because no harm to anyone was done, and my supervisee set a precedent. I also think that the Board knew under umbrella supervision I could indeed supervise my supervisee.

My victory was however very short lived. Once again, the State Board called me in. This time they decimated me. I was furious afterward at the incredible injustice.

I remember talking to an 80-year-old retired psychologist who once said to me, "Psychology has lost its humanity."

He was so right. There was no decency or common sense left, and if The State Board and subsequent organizations do not have it then all is indeed inhumane. If we refuse to fight for the dignity of truth, then we have substituted expediency for justice. This was a quote from a Perry Mason episode. I'm thinking where is Perry Mason when you need him?

About this time, I was also supervising a doctoral intern. Even his professor at school stated his supervision by me was, "excellent" and he got an "A" in his internship. The Board never however asked for my notes on him. They never asked anything about him at all. About that time my doctoral intern felt uncomfortable with the secretary, who had a conflictual relationship with her own son, and wanted to "adopt" my doctoral intern as a surrogate son. She called him a lot even when he went on vacation with his fiancé. He reported this to me and I had a talk with her about it. I found she was also breaking confidentiality with my patients about others. She also did not like my wife setting limits with her and one day brought in "Bitch Be Gone" pills from a novelty shop. The implication was clear. She told patients that my wife was indeed a bitch. She also told my supervisee that she and I would make a good pair and that we should dump our spouses and have sex in the office while she would act as a lookout. I had known my supervisee for a while and she was a devout Christian. There was never a sexual affair between us, nor would there be. She then went down to the other counselors in the facility and told them that I was having sex with my supervisee, and other women in the practice. A counselor who I have known for over ten years told me what she was doing. Again, I thought of what Dr. Mark told me about her being a Borderline Personality. I felt her sting. My wife could not figure out how I attract such dysfunctional women.

I brought her into my office but I did not close the door completely, thank goodness. The counselor who told me about what my secretary was doing was eavesdropping. I do not condone this but in my case, it was a saving grace. She heard the whole conversation. I asked the secretary why she was doing this to me. I told her that what she was saying to the staff was all lies.

She stated bluntly, "Yes, I know but I'm believable."

I again said, "But I gave you a job when you did not have one, I don't get it."

She put it out there and said, "I'm jealous of you because everyone likes you and you and the rest are college educated, and everyone is having fun while I'm stuck up in front. Your supervisee is beautiful and my sister is pretty and always got all the attention. Even my son hates me."

Again, hurt people, hurt people. I softened but what she did was beyond belief. My wife came in soon afterward and after I discussed what happened she fired her on the spot. The counselor told my wife and I that she had heard everything and if this went to court she would tell everything she heard. I told her that perhaps this was the end of it, but unfortunately it was not. It was the beginning of the Apocalypse.

The trauma therapist I hired then went off on me a week later. She accused me of "ripping her off" in terms of insurance reimbursements. I had to answer to the law for this and was exonerated. She then told me why she was truly angry at me, as explained before she was angry that I fired her "best friend" my secretary. She went as well. I found out that other counselors listened to her and they all reported me to The Great and Powerful Psychology Board for Fraud. Again, the Board found no Fraud issues and I was, for the umpteenth time, exonerated on any Fraud. As I found out later this counselor accused one of my colleagues of the same thing, and my colleague was exonerated. She said to me, "some people are just bad eggs to quote Willy Wonka."

The State Board, per their lead investigator contacted my doctoral intern telling him that there was an investigation on me. Even he wondered why they should contact him as his internship had ended.

He stated to me in a quizzical way, "Should this be brought to me, I mean isn't this confidential?"

I told him that I did not know what is confidential and what is not. I did talk to the Social Work and Counselor Board concerning my supervisee.

They told me that this, "State Psychology Board is not always very ethical and that they do try to avoid contact with them. Furthermore, they told me that "with them nothing is confidential." This was troubling in that it came from another Board. How one Board view things as confidential but another Board does not is a mystery. Is not the law the same for both Boards in relation to confidentiality?

The State Board wanted to know who all the women were in my practice. They asked the intern to divulge this. When he asked why, they stated because his past secretary had been in contact with the State Board and reported him for sexual exploitation of his supervisee. This investigator then asked him, per the Executive Director of the State Board, not to inform me of the conversation they were having. He liked me and felt strongly that I was being framed. Soon after, my secretary had called him telling the Board that she felt I was very amoral and unethical in having sex with my supervisee. She also told this intern that I told the Board that she tried to stop me but I refused to listen. This was all fabricated by a vengeful woman.

The intern stated "I had known him for a year and saw no impropriety whatsoever in the practice by Dr. Tom."

He told me she then said, "I know but I wanted to get back at him for firing me."

He called me up and told me the whole thing. I was sick at my stomach. I told him that my career was gone, because The Board's Executive Director did not like me anyway because I challenged him at my last interrogation, and obviously did not trust me. I thought, *so much for objectivity.*

He said he would testify in my defense if I needed. He did not like my secretary because she attempted to "mother me" he said. He reported that he felt smothered by her. About three weeks or so my attorney got another letter from the Board wanting me back. We talked about what the intern had told me and my lawyer talked to the Board. They told him since that had no real proof of anything they just wanted to talk more to me about my supervision. There would be nothing of a sexual nature asked.

Again, I found myself in front of the State Board for another three hours of grueling questions concerning sexual exploitation of my supervisee that they told my lawyer they would not ask. They would not tell me who said what or who accused me of what.

"You don't have any right to know your accusers", the Executive Director belted out.

I now knew what those innocent people felt at the Salem Witch Trials. As a matter of fact, one lawyer told me afterward that this States Board was a "Kangaroo Court" and basically you do not have too much of a chance even if you are innocent. I'm thinking this is the 21st century and these things still happen---apparently, they do. I found out that the Board only talked to the females that were let go, because the Executive Director felt, in his twisted logic, that the women who were let go would tell the truth because they now have nothing to lose. Ummmm, perhaps because they were let go they just might have an axe to grind, and acted in concert---just a thought. I'm sure my ex-secretary would absolutely be honest---not! She said she was a devout Christian. I think God will love her too.

Then I learned that my intern and my ex-secretary was questioned by the Board and taped.

They told my intern that they had no evidence but wanted to know "If he felt I could have done this."

To which he told me that he said, "You are asking subjective questions, not objectively fact based questions."

Furthermore, he told me that they felt that Dr. Tom may have done this but had no direct proof other than what the secretary stated. They wanted support from him.

He said that, "Dr. Tom was always appropriate."

In the meantime, the lead investigator quietly took my supervisee to lunch to talk to her about my sexual exploitation. Again, she denied this and told her that the secretary was very deceitful and told her that she would make up lies to get her in trouble because she was jealous. She became tearful and avoided coming to work for a few days. I, to this day cannot understand how cruel people can be. They are obviously motivated by self interest.

During my second questioning the Director again tore into me for three hours.

He asked questions like, "So you were caught coming out of your supervisee's office with lipstick on your collar."

To which I replied, "That would be amazing since I have known her for a few years now and never saw her put lipstick on, and. to my knowledge she does not use it."

Another question was, "You had a doctor writing prescriptions in your office and do you know why he left?"

I replied, "Yes, he left because he was not making as much money as he wanted." "No!" the Executive Director stated in anger. "It was because you were having sex with your supervisee."

I replied in frustration with a tinge of anger, "Then why did he put in writing that he left because of financial reasons."

I replied "You told me during our first go around that if something is not in writing then it does not exist, are you now amending your own rule?"

The Executive Director said nothing but I did see his anger boil slowly. My lawyer again whispered to me to basically say nothing for they have all the power and by contradicting him and the Board I am signing my death warrant. So, this is American Justice, so where's Bill Kurtis? I then asked the Executive Director if he asked "everyone" in my practice about me and these alleged practices.

He replied succinctly, "Yes everyone."

I inquired as to two other female staff that was still with my practice and they told me they never heard from the Board. The Executive Director obviously lied. I wonder, is that ethical? Who will restrict him? My supervisee told me about the meeting with the investigator. She said to her that she personally felt there was no violation and the only violations were the minor ones from the first meeting. There was no harm, but the Executive Director felt otherwise and did not trust me even though they had no proof. She also stated that the Board should genuinely allow me to continue to supervise based upon the rules. She even offered to help us out about finding ways to make the practice more profitable. This is what my supervisee told me what the investigator told her. I felt relief, but it was short lived. After my session with the Board I felt a bit fearful because I now knew how they operated. It was a bit scary. I held my breath for a few weeks until they sent forth a "consent agreement". If I signed it, I could keep my license if I refused they would pull my license forever. My lawyer did not go over the agreement or the possible consequences. He urged me to sign it. When I read, it I was stupefied. My wife and I read it over several times and I told my lawyer it was full of half-truths and outright lies- not the whole truth and it was biased. My lawyer never told me I could write a refutation as part of the record. So all people see is the consent agreement but not my refutation or my response.

Even a Yiddish proverb states, "A half-truth is a whole lie."

Furthermore, Abraham Lincoln said, "A lie which is a half-truth is ever the blackest of lies."

My lawyer nervously said, "I know but sign it anyway or they will pull your license."

I refused to sign it and on the last minute on the last hour my lawyer pleaded with me again to sign, saying essentially that if I did not sign you will lose your license and they will never give it back. I broke down and signed it. Cutting my throat would have been more merciful. I am filled with frustration at the State Board and this profession for their unjust, non- restorative practices, bending of rules and despite their policy saying that they are all about restoration and rehabilitation, their inhumanity. Boards like the one in this state are a black stain on the integrity of a profession that is judged to be humane by society. They gave me a Permanent Restriction for the rest of my career to ever supervise anyone again, basically cutting my throat career wise. I found out through talking with lawyers that Boards have been given too much latitude in terms of use of "administrative law". This denies certain rights to individuals, like their use of hearsay, not being able to present evidence because they do not have to look at it. Nor do you have a right to confidentiality or knowing you accuser. Even Jesus could confront his accusers. At least my Board conducted itself this way. They told me I could bring it to a hearing and present evidence, and when I suggested to my lawyer to do this – he told me we would lose because the court system would almost always support the Boards. He reminded me that I did commit some paper violations. I told him I was completely honest, and it is like putting to death someone who ran a stop sign and no one was killed. He agreed but told me if I did not sign the" half-baked" consent agreement then they had the right to take my license, as they can do it and I would never get it back. Under this threat, I signed, much to my wife's dismay. At least I still had a license, but realized later it basically sealed any opportunities for active employment. One incident destroyed over twenty-five years of ethical service based upon administrative law, pathological, prejudiced people who sit on a State "Ethical" Board. They bend the rules to their liking without repercussions and feel free to make these value decisions on professional lives. I told my wife I stand by what I have said. She hugged me and told me she will stand with me too.

Thus, my practice folded. I lost a job as a contractor for nursing homes that I had for seven years. I could not buy a job. Insurance companies dried up on me with many not willing to renew their contracts with me. Clients never returned, friends and colleagues walked away from me. No referrals came, and the trauma therapist spread more lies about me in the community. When I wanted to sue her for defamation I could not find a lawyer willing to take the case. When I asked other lawyers I either could not afford them or they said I did not have a case. They disagreed on the law---some saying I had a case others saying I did not. Some lawyers even misquoted the law. I am very paranoid of our justice system now. I now know why Shakespeare told us that the first thing we must do is to kill all the lawyers. Why can't we do the right thing? I also received a judgment against me because I could not pay my biller the money I owed her. I wonder why? I am fighting my way through a myriad of financial issues now. Thank you, "Ethical State Board, of Psychology". I will not let this destroy me however, and I realize that despite these problems life is still so very beautiful and I am grateful to be alive. I will persevere somehow. I know I have helped a lot of people and no one ever committed suicide on my watch. I will still help in any capacity any person I can help. This will give me an opportunity to do more volunteer work, because we are all here only for a visit as my dad once said, and I still want to make the most of my time. Hopefully, when my time comes people will recall the good I did. People ask me if I hate the State Board as many psychologists do, and I tell them that if I stay angry I keep myself a prisoner. If God exists, they must answer for what they have done. I'm looking forward to a new chapter in my life now. I am not sure where the winds will take me now. I was looking for an out and they provided it to me.

I was looking out of my window one Saturday night at my home. It was raining so hard that a little bird was so waterlogged outside my door that he could not fly. I pulled him in and dried him off, convincing him or me that everything would be alright. I went over and put him in my garage. I went out to my porch and just looked up as the rain came down, and laughed as hard as I was being drenched. Thank goodness, my wife was in bed or she would have called an ambulance. I thought about how self-centered I had been. There are so many people in America who struggle every day: the elderly in nursing homes who have a host of medical issues, and have lost functioning or cannot get the help financially they need. I thought about men and women who have suffered in the Holocaust. Or those war veterans like Mr. Louis Zamperini, who was tortured by the Japanese in World War –Two and transcended his experience. The poor in America who do not know where their next meal will come from, or felons who want to go straight and cannot catch a break after their release. The rain that night echoed my tears, which was beguiled by my laughter.

It was at that time that my anger at a dysfunctional Executive Director and State Board subsided. Two days later I had an even deeper experience which helped me heal. A Board member came to me for a pain assessment evaluation.

He knew of my case and said, "I'm from the State Board and I know what happened to you."

At first, I told him how angry I was at the unfairness and the injustice. Surprisingly enough, he agreed with me. He told me that this board was the most hated board in this state. He agreed subtly that power could be abused and basically as a lawyer agreed they collected "scalps". He told me quietly how the Executive Director could be and the Board and how they could violate their own policies. Believe it or not this helped validate my thoughts and feelings and was therapeutic. He apologized for what happened to me and I sympathized with him. He was planning to leave the board himself at some point. He told me to challenge them again, but I told him the legal system tends to support these administrative agencies even when they do harm. He agreed stating indeed that they have a "whole lot of immunity around them." He still encouraged me to try. I mellowed considerably and told him that if I hold on to my anger all I do is hold me prisoner to my own fears and hurt. He agreed and encouraged me to let it go. He told me to think about it. I have been an ethical psychologist for near thirty years, and then you meet a punitive and dysfunctional state board, so people believe in them, that does not mean they are right or just however. People just do not know what really goes on but they work off perceptions. After all, we are brought up trusting in our systems, and it is only when we see the human factor and the harm that comes from it that one gets a new perspective. I asked him why they would do this because they are supposing to model ethical behaviors that instill themes of integrity and values. He told me it always comes down to money, power and status. I thanked him for his decency and honesty and I came out with a different point of view. I did his assessment and wished him the very best and he wished me well.

About a month later, my "new" lawyer called and told me something weird happened.

I said with a pain in my chest, "I'm not sure what you are talking about?"

He replied, "The Psychology Board may be dismantled and will be refreshed."

I replied loudly, "What!"

He told me that he could not understand it, something happened. He told me this could be good for me in terms of having this restriction removed. He would get back to me. I broke down and after hanging up just sat quietly in my office. Will miracles never cease? I wondered if the board member that I talked to had anything to do with this. I was not sure what was happening, but as of this writing it is still in strong consideration for change. I am hopeful. Even if this happens and I am released from the bondage of this restriction, I have decided to leave the profession I worked so very hard in. I think this best now, as my disillusionment will interfere with optimal treatment. I might be burning out now as well. Maybe I will be more a political advocate for mental health, I do not know, where I will go or what I will do. I had recently written letters to congressmen hoping to facilitate change or give my plight a voice.

I went home and told my wife what happened and she hugged me tightly with tears in her eyes. I then went to the garage but forgot about the bird I had rescued and imprisoned there. I lifted the garage door and he flew around for a while, landed on one of my fishing poles, as if contemplating the fact that he would be free from this restraint. He then flew out; he was free-at last. He was alive again and free as perhaps I.

I went back in thinking about life and learning that life is only temporary and if we can love and help each other than life becomes a bit easier and tolerable.

My father once told me, "That we are all here only for a visit, and if we can learn to cooperate, like we did in the Army, then things will go much better."

He went on to say that when you think about it people create their own problems, and there is really no such thing as an accident, it comes when we act in a selfish manner as opposed to working cooperatively. He told me that when you see the monument to the Marines who raised the flag on Mount Sarabachi, it was not one man. This represented teamwork to reach a goal. Therefore, America becomes so productive because it is not about the one but the many. I miss the wisdom my father eschewed. He sadly passed away suddenly before he could ever see the dream of this document come to fruition, and his inspiration for it.

The great thing about America is that everywhere you look there are heroes. These ordinary people do great things everyday but are not always recognized for their heroism. These are the unsung heroes which make this country great. I read somewhere about a New York City policeman buying boots for a homeless man, or the fireman who rushes in a burning house to rescue a child. These are the unsung heroes which make America Great. I believe it is stated on the monument: "Uncommon valor was a common virtue."

An old Chinese proverb goes somewhat like this: "To truly understand others is to be knowledgeable, but to truly understand yourself is to be wise."

Ben once told me that I was on a similar quest. He was right. The quest was about "self-discovery" and finding out how wise we were about ourselves, getting past the pretenses, material gains and items and coming down to the care of our humanity and the purpose in our lives. As I grow in this field, I am coming more to terms with myself and what I am about in relation to our social context.

Louis Carroll once wrote, "All that we have is what we give to others."

A famous actor who I admire once made a comment, now that he is in his "golden years," that basically one's life can be better measured "not by the quantity of it, but rather the quality" we put in it. Time is precious and it is a fleeting commodity. One must make the best of time.

I sometimes envision myself sitting in a wheelchair in a nursing home, probably drooling, with a young twenty-year-old LPN who has decided to park me in a corner somewhere and leave me in my stinky Depends while she talks about her latest date to other young LPNs or nurses' aides. Then I think so what is the sum existence of a person's life. What is the measure of a man or woman? Perhaps we are basically judged by who we are and what we have done, hopefully in the spirit of giving and helping others.

Of course, given managed care, and the economy, I won't be able to retire. I'll probably be doing group therapy with the other nursing home patients, providing any of us, of course, still have a mind left. Even if there is one neuron firing in my brain by then, so to speak, I would like to think I can both entertain and pass on some wise passage to that young LPN who has parked me against a blond wall while she does her thing. Of course, I might also decide to chase her around the facility in my wheel chair – ha!!! Therefore, we can make the best and most of a situation as hopefully we have choices to some degree. I was fortunate to have brilliant teachers who studied alongside the great names in psychology: Dr. Abraham Maslow, Dr. Carl Rogers, Dr. Rudolph Driekers, Carl Whitaker, etc. It was more than just learning "techniques or strategies," it was learning about me, humanity and having gentleness for all things living. A young therapist who was very angry once asked me if he would become a very competent therapist. I told him the potential was there, but not now. He asked me why I felt this way and I told him because he had yet to understand and transcend his own anger. Anger is not something to necessarily fear, although it can become volatile. It is something to understand, embrace, and come to terms with because it is about that person, unmet needs, fear, anxiety and a degree of powerlessness. To come to terms with ourselves, flaws and all is a very powerful thing. Ben once taught me that as therapists we deal with transitional issues all the time, and that good constructive psychotherapy is highly relational and "a healing" for both parties. Being mindful to oneself in therapy is so crucial and Ben always taught me that as a therapist, you will always be in supervision, even with yourself (mindfulness). Even after being in the field of mental health for twenty years, I've discovered there is truly so much more I do not know about myself or others. Someone once asked me if I was afraid of death. Dr. Carl Rogers once looked upon it yet another growth experience when queried about it at a seminar. If God truly exists, I would rather like to have a lengthy discussion with him. If he doesn't, I guess I don't have to worry, because it doesn't matter then. Coming to terms with mortality is something we all must do at some point. I had an experience which helped me work through this to some degree.

I rented a Piper Cherokee 180 aircraft. (For those of you who are pilots or familiar with aircraft, you will know the type of plane, others will need to Google a picture). Being a relatively low time pilot at the time, I dismissed with some of the weather briefs (big mistake). Even though at the airport I was taking off from the sun was out and there were no clouds in the sky, at my destination airport and an hour away, the clouds hung low, it was overcast and hazing up. I took off thinking I could make it and called ahead at another airport on the way to my destination airport. Weather was holding, but closing. Discretion was the better part of valor, but I showed fool-hardy courage and plowed on into the wild, very wild blue yonder. Suddenly and unexpectedly, I found myself at 3000 feet and descending into a cloud - a very big cumulous cloud – not a good or legal thing to do for a novice VFR (visual flight rules) pilot. I was taught as a rule to do a 180° turn out of the cloud. I did that. The cloud was endless. It was like being in a steam bath with the steam so thick you couldn't even see your hand three feet in front of you. Suddenly, my autonomic nervous system went into hyper drive and I was instantly bathed in sweat. I don't know why, but the words "immediate death" was etched on my brain. I started too actually panic. Fear took over; I lost all sense of logic and spatial-visual awareness. I was essentially horrified. I banked the aircraft more than 70 degrees. I don't know how I didn't fall out of the sky or stall out and enter a spin. I climbed, descended, and turned crazily looking for an out. My emotional brain was taking over. All logic went out the window. I thought death will come quick. I'll just impact the ground and I'll be scattered over 10 states. Then amazingly I thought, *God, if I crash, will you let me not come down on a school yard or other residential area. I couldn't live with that if I did live.* Then, as if a divine miracle happened, the stall warning light and buzzer came to life on the instrument panel and woke me up. I suddenly remembered what my flight instructor taught me. I could see his face.

"If you ever find yourself in instrument conditions (minimal visibility), go on instruments only. Do not trust your senses."

This was like a mystical experience for me. Suddenly I looked at all the gauges, leveled out the aircraft, put cruise power back in, watched my airspeed (which is life to a pilot), and rate of climb and attitude (pitch) of the airplane. Slowly, I talked to myself, thanked God and my instructor, and slowly ascended to 6000 feet climbing out of the cloud. I was grateful there were no other planes in my cloud. I set up a course for my home airport while talking with a nearby control tower that set up flight following (watching my flight route for other aircraft). Upon landing, which I gently bounced in, I taxied up and saw a line mechanic wave to me. When I parked the plane, and turned off the engine, I leapt out so fast and instantly made love to the ground, kissing it passionately.

The mechanic came over and said "Hey Doc, are you ok?"

I said, "I am now! "Life is good, don't you think?"

He replied, "Sure Doc, whatever you say," and looked at me rather funny like all psychologists are a bit off center anyway.

I guess he had never seen a guy kiss the ground before. I had not flown again for a month after that experience, but decided, however, that I couldn't let that fear overtake me and I went up with my instructor getting additional training and getting over my fear of piloting a plane again. That experience was very existential for me somehow, but thus, my fear for death had decreased and I realized it is part of the natural order of things, although I don't want to ever push it again, so to speak. Since that time, I've measured any aversive experience against that and remain in some degree in self-control emotionally, even under stress.

This has benefited others who say "How can you remain so calm?"

"Because I flew in a cloud," I say.

They are completely confused. Life experiences can be our greatest teachers, but they are sometimes very difficult instructors.

As I have heard it said, "Life gives the exam first then the lesson".

Sometimes I wish there was a "do-over" button like in those children's games we used to play. If we feel things are unfair or didn't turn out right, we would yell "do-over." Maybe there would be a button – a do-over button. I'll bet there would be millions of people pushing the do-over button. For example, a woman looking at her life with her lazy, womanizing, wife beating alcoholic husband might just push the do-over button, but this is just a guess. I wonder what the world would be like with do-over buttons.

It's truly ironic that man and woman with his/her ingenuity, intelligence and determination have built up such a beautiful world: skyscrapers, increasingly better technology and modes of transportation like space travel. Yet we continue to squabble with each other, have domestic issues, kill each other, emotionally torture each other, cheat on each other, and find different ways to hurt ourselves. Both Sigmund Freud and Carl Jung discussed the duality of man – the pleasure, the pain, the brilliance, the stupidity, the selflessness and the selfishness. These components are within all of us and ultimately it always seems to come down to the choices we make as people based on our own perceptions of our own goals at the time. Are they, per Alfred Adler, a fiction and self-serving, or are they other centered fostering social interest and cooperation. As a team, we build skyscrapers, but it takes only one terrorist to bring it down who has his or her own self-serving bias. Scary thought – food for thought perhaps. I have visited the pediatric units of hospitals talking to mothers experiencing post-partum depression. I've looked at the variety of new babies through the glass in their cribs with their blue or pink hats on. I wonder what they will grow up like. Or, what world will they see, what will they integrate and assimilate from their parents and environment. How they grow up to help or hurt mankind? Every child is our future, our destiny and I believe we have the moral imperative to nurture, support and encourage our children to be the best they can and be productive citizens helping to make our world a better place for everyone. This, however, is complex issue given genetics, environments, biology, parenting issues, etc. We, as parents can only do our best and hope for the best, and we will all make mistakes, as we are but human. The goal is to learn from them however, if we do not than that is the true failure, and heartbreak.

Psychology permeates every aspect of our being whether we acknowledge it or not, as does sociology, history and biology. There are always everyday heroisms by common people shown, and this is truly a great thing. Even the little things can make a great difference in a person's life. If I had the power to change things in mental health I would require: A serious look at how managed care can be redefined and focus more on quality not always higher premiums at the expense of cost cutting measures. I would give personality tests to all students entering this field. They would also be required to undergo counseling in a term even if they need it or not. Better research is needed with greater sample populations and specific populations with good outcome studies. Focusing on the clinicians in the trenches so to speak rather than just compiling research for academic sake. Our State Boards must be reexamined so they are held to the highest standards of accountability. They should be reviewed and when unjust practices occur, and they do, then another independent review Board could act as an oversight to insure integrity and justice, checks and balances. Personality tests should be given to them as well to determine fitness for duty. Unless you have a great lawyer, who is willing to fight for justice, you might as well throw in the towel. If your guilty it is one thing, but if innocent one needs to fight for justice. Boards can become way overzealous. Not all Boards are unjust thank goodness. Let's study the Story of Captain John McVay, the skipper of the famed Indianapolis ship. It was sunk in the Pacific Ocean in 1945. This illustrates how Administrative Boards can create unbelievable destruction. I saw the movie "Sulley" and saw what the NTSB Board tried to do with Chesley Sullenberger and identified with him in a strange way. I felt a bit traumatized by it. I saw the potential "railroading" of this amazing hero by this Board and it again angered me and disillusioned me. I had a flashback. When are we ever going to do the right thing? As was stated in the film, they should have pinned a medal on the man.

I would not look at gun control as much as to expand mental health education to the public so the signs may be seen for people, before they go on shooting rampages. This is only my opinion. As I had said before the mentally impaired or criminal minded do not care about gun control, they get guns. Yes, we do need to protect ourselves and families, but I have felt that mental health seems lacking too much. This is a complex issue however, and my opinion may be debated. Mental health needs to be on par with medical services, in my opinion. I do abhor violence. The parity issue has holes in it when it comes to mental health. The government and the populace must take mental health very seriously. We can't just think our way out of schizophrenia or Bipolar disorder, I wish we could. Mental health matters. We need more education and more funding in mental health not funding cuts. When it hits someone with power and influence it seems that is the only time it becomes an issue. Why can it not be an issue before it turns into a tragedy for some family? We can work hard as a nation to curb some of these tragedies, maybe not all but even one life that is saved because someone saw the sign is indeed worth it. Our veterans need help as well and good quality service. The problems with veterans have been going on way to long. I have counseled many vets and many complain about availability and quality of services. My dad was a World War Two vet, and he was wounded. I honor him and all the vets who fought to keep America Magnificent and Free in no matter what war. We owe them everything we can give them. We need to do more to curb the drug problem which is eating our youth. On one morning talk show I was shocked to hear how a particular State wanted to cut funding for treatment programs that deal with the ever-increasing heroin problem. This is exactly what I am talking about, do not cut funding for an epidemic issue, but enhance effectiveness for treatment. Make our youth strong again and productive, as they are our future. Addictions are an epidemic and we need more dually diagnosed programs, and adequately trained counselors. We may not prevent all these types of tragedies but we might be able to reduce them. I am hoping that change is in the wind now, and people, governments and professional organizations take heed. America is great but we need, in my opinion, to pull together as a country. There is no better time than now.

In his wonderful book, "The Self Esteem Workbook," by Dr. Glenn R. Schiraldi, Dr. Schiraldi goes on to quote W.T. Gallwey (1974), "The Inner Game of Tennis."

He cites the passage, "When we plant a rose seed in the earth, we notice that it is small, but we do not criticize it as 'rootless and stemless.' We treat it as a seed, giving it the water and nourishment required of a seed. When it first shoots up out of the earth, we don't condemn it as an immature and underdeveloped, nor do we criticize the buds for not being open when they appear. We stand in wonder at the process taking place and give the plant the care it needs at each stage of its development. The rose is a rose from the time it is a seed to the time it dies. Within it, at all times, it contains its whole potential. It seems to be constantly in the process of change; yet at each state, at each moment, it is [whole] as it is."

I hope this book brought the reader laughter, thought, hope, courage, inspiration and above all: a realization that life is truly both a miracle and a gift not to be thrown away lightly, or cast asunder. As I grow older, how we treat each other becomes ever so more important. It is greater than all the wealth in the world. I'll leave the reader with a final thought.

Emily Dickinson once wrote, "If I can stop one heart from breaking, I shall not live in vain. If I can ease one life in aching, or cool one pain, or help one fainting robin unto his nest again, I shall not live in vain."

So, is there a pill for that?

Printed in the United States
By Bookmasters